GSHADOW GUARDIAN

AND THE BIG BAD WOLF

SHADOW GUARDIAN SERIES

SHADOW GUARDIAN
AND THE BIG BAD WOLF

ROBERT J. LEWIS

4 Horsemen
Publications, Inc.

4 Horsemen
Publications, Inc.

4 Horsemen Publications, Inc.
1497 Main St. Suite 169
Dunedin, FL 34698
4horsemenpublications.com
info@4horsemenpublications.com

Cover and Typeset by Autumn Skye
Editor Kristine Cotter

Library of Congress Control Number: 2023932319

Print ISBN: 978-1-64450-855-8
Hardcover ISBN: 978-1-64450-856-5
Ebook ISBN: 978-1-64450-857-2
Audio ISBN: 978-1-64450-858-9

Of course, I dedicate this to my beloved mom and dad, Dolores C. Lewis and Robert O. Lewis. I also have to dedicate this to my writing task master and diva dog, Bonita. To Randy, Chris, William, Jeff, Berto, Rodney, Brian, and Kalvin. Your love, support, and encouragement mean the world to me. Last but not least, you, the readers. Without you, I wouldn't be where I am today.

In this story, we have Elias. Elias is transgendered, but because of the time period they grew up in, they weren't able to live their truth. It took me some time to decide what pronouns to use for them. Using he/him felt wrong and insulting to the character. I thought about using she/her, but I felt that would get confusing to you, the reader. I finally decided to use the neutral pronouns of they/them. This way, I wasn't misgendering a character that I love, and I wasn't confusing you, the reader.

TABLE OF CONTENTS

CHAPTER 1

E LIAS SKIPPED MERRILY DOWN THE
dirt road to Don Marcos's farm. Even though
the man and his lands sent shivers down Elias's
spine, they were happy to be away from everyone
so they could be themself. They treasured these
moments when they did not need to pretend to be
something they were not. These moments were
rare and grew farther and fewer as they grew older.

For as long as Elias could remember, they felt
off, as if they were born into the wrong body. They
also learned early on not to say such things out
loud. The first time someone heard them say it,
they ended up with their father's belt across their
backside. The second was their mother's wooden
spoon. Both times had earned them a lecture that
saying such things in public could have dire consequences for them and their family.

The Tribunal of the Holy Office of the Inquisition was always on the watch for anyone that did not live up to their holy piety standard. A woman and her newborn child were taken because a local priest said the child's birthmark was the sign of the devil. Don Octavio, the elderly widower that was too sick and weak to attend church, was dragged out of his home and burned at the stake for heresy.

"I know you're different. I'm different, too," their cousin Francisco told them privately one day. "Not like you, but I am. With Queen Isabella and King Ferdinand driving the Moors from Spain, it's a dangerous time for people like us and our families."

Elias understood but did not like it.

"Maybe one day," Francisco added wistfully, "people like us will be able to live freely and openly."

"But not today," Elias finished.

Francisco tousled Elias's curly hair. "No, not today, but someday." Someday couldn't come soon enough for Elias.

With times growing harder by the day, Francisco had found work as a stable hand for Don Marcos, and Elias had been quietly tasked with taking Francisco his afternoon meal while the rest of the world took their siesta. Elias didn't mind. They got to be themself, even if they didn't quite understand who that was yet.

Elias continued down the road, keeping an eye out for any of the wild dogs that freely roamed in packs on Don Marcos's lands. Their bloodthirsty howls could be heard for miles around, and Elias would often see them stalking them in the tall grasses by the road. They never stepped on the road, but Elias was always ready to run if that ever changed.

Today they were eerily quiet and the grasses didn't move with their prowling. That unsettled Elias. In the six months they had traveled down this dirt road, the wild dogs always made themselves known. Elias's abuela used to tell him that it was the threats you didn't see, the hidden ones, which were the most dangerous.

Elias froze. The tall grass ahead of them rustled. Elias swallowed down their fear. Gingerly, they took a step forward. The rustling in the grass moved closer. Each terror-filled step Elias made, the rustling in the grass matched. Three more steps, and they would be side by side.

Taking in a deep breath, Elias was ready to turn and run. They raised their foot to take another step. The grass rippled. Elias's heart pounded with fear. Watching the grass move, Elias slowly lowered their foot. The grass stopped moving. A trickle of sweat ran down Elias's face. Pressing their foot to the ground, Elias let out his breath when nothing happened.

Elias's relief was short-lived. Something shot out from the grass too fast for Elias to see. Closing their eyes, they fell back, screaming in fear. Falling on their butt, Elias started kicking and flailing their arms in the air, hoping to strike whatever was attacking them. Only they hit nothing.

Elias stopped their thrashing. Opening one eye, then the other, Elias peered down past their feet. Sitting there, flapping its tail back and forth while looking at them curiously, was an orange and white barn cat. Elias couldn't help the laughter that escaped them when they righted themself.

"What are you doing out here?" Elias asked, dusting themself off as they stood.

The cat cocked its head to the side, then let out a question, "Meow?"

"Don't you know there are wild dogs around here that would eat you?" Elias asked the cat.

The cat righted its head, then stood and stretched. It let out an unimpressed "meow" before strolling over to Elias and running through their legs.

"I don't have time for this. Go on, get," Elias said, annoyed.

Elias reached down to move the cat, but it quickly darted away, running ahead of them. It stopped and turned around with its tail dancing in the air. The cat let out an impatient "meow."

"I don't have time to play your games. Go home," Elias scolded the feline.

The cat let out another impatient "meow." This one more urgent than the first.

Elias started back down the road, intending to ignore the bothersome furball as they passed by. The cat, however, had other ideas, turning around and heading down the road ahead of Elias.

At first, the cat kept pace with Elias. Every so often, it would let out a commanding "meow," then pick up speed until it was running down the road.

Not even realizing it, Elias had matched the feline's speed and was blindly chasing after the cat. The cat led them off the road and into the grasses. The cat stopped at a ditch that ran along the road. Elias did not have time to panic that they had strayed from the safety of the road. They were taken aback by the sight of a beautiful woman, a Gitana, lying in the ditch, her flowing, jet-black hair and colorful dress splayed out around her.

The cat sat next to her, letting out a mournful "meow."

"Do not fret; my dear Felix." The Gitana raised a trembling hand to stroke the cat, her gold bracelets glinted in the sun. She coughed, sending a trickle of blood escaping from the corner of her mouth. "It will be okay. I have seen it." She turned her emerald green eyes to Elias.

Elias forgot to be afraid as they marveled at her beauty. In awe, Elias asked, "Do you need me to get help?"

Her ruby-red lips formed a warm smile. She reached out with her other hand to Elias. "My, aren't you a beautiful young lady. Come here, so I can get a better look at you."

Elias didn't correct her. It somehow felt right. They stepped forward to take her hand. A strange tingling flowed from the Gitana into Elias. Elias knelt beside her. They could feel her staring deep inside them.

"I see you. The real you," the Gitana explained. "And I'm sorry to tell you that you'll be reborn many times before you are able to make your outsides match what is inside you."

Her words terrified Elias. "I should go get help."

"I am sorry, my darling, to pass this burden onto you as well. I am the last of my family." The Gitana released Elias's hand and placed her fingertips on their forehead. "You are not of my blood, but you are of my kind. With my family gone, my soul has no tether to this mortal plane."

Elias felt the surge of knowledge flowing into them, unlocking the doors of potential and revealing hidden truths. "My companion, Felix, will guide and protect you in this life and in the ones to come."

Elias heard the cat meow mournfully. "You must stop the demon, Don Marcos, before he feasts on yet another innocent young man's soul." The Gitana removed her hand from Elias's forehead.

From the folds of her skirt, she produced a curved dagger in its sheath. She pressed it into Elias's hand. Then she lifted her head slightly and removed a golden necklace with a medallion from around her neck.

"This amulet of power will always find its way back to you. It is your connection to us," she explained, closing Elias's hand around the charm. "I will guide you until my last breath in the battle ahead. Go now, my brave sister. Put an end to Don Marcos and save your cousin."

"Francisco." Elias stood, their eyes widening with alarm. "I'll come back for you, I promise."

Slipping the jewelry on and tucking the dagger into their belt, Elias tore off running through the tall grass. Once back on the road, Elias pushed themself to go faster. Felix appeared beside them, keeping pace.

CHAPTER 2

DIEGO SILENTLY CURSED. JUAN Carlos had Freddy and him in the garden rearranging plants under the hot late-summer sun. Esmerelda was going to start growing her herbs in Juan Carlos's garden, and she had very specific criteria for growing her plants. Diego would have complained, but he had a lingering fear she'd give him a tail.

With his hands on his hips, Diego took a moment to catch his breath and ponder. Juan Carlos's answers as to why Esmerelda and Freddy were his backups at the gym had been cryptic, enigmatic at best. He couldn't confront Freddy or Esmerelda about it without revealing his secret, though Diego had an inkling they already knew.

A white towel hit Diego in the face. "Daydreaming again?" Freddy laughed. He had a massive concrete planter that was too heavy for Diego to move on his own, balanced on one shoulder. "Man, I haven't seen you this sweaty since I used to train you when we were kids."

"You mean when you used to toss me across the room and called it training?" Diego said bitterly, wiping his brow. "Do you need help with that?"

"Naw, I'm good," Freddy said cockily. "Hey! Juan Carlos, where do you want this?"

"Over on the east side, so it gets the morning sun." Juan Carlos strolled up, sipping a glass of ice water. He eyed Diego. "Diego, why are you just standing around? Esmerelda needs those bags of manure moved to her part of the garden."

Diego pouted. "Can't Freddy do it? I don't want to stink when Alex gets here."

"What's next?" Freddy asked, strolling up casually. He leaned in and sniffed Diego. "You smell."

Diego glared at Freddy. "Not cool, man."

"He also had sex with a man," Freddy said, crinkling his nose.

Diego gawked at Freddy. "Dude!"

"Diego, go move the manure," Juan Carlos ordered, trying not to laugh. "Federico, come with me. I have some heavy stone planters that need moving."

Diego whined as they walked away, "Why can't I move the planters?"

"He needs muscle," Freddy called back, flexing his sinewy biceps.

"I'm twice your size!" Diego yelled back. Sulking, Diego kicked the ground. "You know, I'm rich enough to pay someone to do this for us!"

"It builds character!" Juan Carlos shouted back.

Grumbling, Diego stomped off. "Fuck character." He picked up one of the bags and tossed it over his shoulder. "They got me doing the shit work. Literally." Diego crossed the rooftop garden to where the newly built raised garden sat under the shade of banana trees.

Diego made five more trips and was about to lift the last fifty-pound bag when Esmerelda came up to him. "Diego?" she said in a questioning tone. "Thank you for carrying all those bags of manure."

"You're welcome." Diego hefted the last bag up onto his shoulder.

She followed alongside Diego as he made his final trip. "Out of curiosity, you do know you could have used the wheelbarrow, right?"

"Yes." Diego dropped the final bag with the others. "Now," he said, slightly embarrassed. "I didn't think about it."

She looked at him with a slight curl to her lips. "You do that a lot, don't you? Not think, that is. Good thing you're pretty."

Diego puffed out his chest and smiled before he realized what she had said. "Hey, I think."

"I know you do." Esmerelda cupped Diego's face with her perfectly manicured hand. "Sometimes you act without thinking, and one day that may put us on opposite sides." She patted his cheek before withdrawing her hand. "If that happens, I will give you a tail."

"If you give me a tail, so help me—"

"If I give you a tail, I am the only one that can help you." Esmerelda finished. Diego took a step back. "Don't worry. I'll make sure it's fluffy and soft, so Alex likes it."

Diego turned his head to call Juan Carlos for protection, but the shout turned to a baffled, "What the fuck? How is he lifting that by himself?"

Diego couldn't believe his eyes. Freddy had a concrete planter that weighed at least five hundred pounds up in the air, one-handed. Juan Carlos was directing him like the mighty feat was nothing new to him.

He returned his attention to Esmerelda when she spoke. "He works out and eats his vegetables." Before Diego could question her explanation, she ordered, "Now, bring over the potting soil. Remember one bag of manure, then two bags of potting soil. Make sure you hand-mix them together. No metal."

"Got it, but—"

She cut him off. "Oh, and use the wheelbarrow this time. I'm off to fry the potatoes." Esmerelda glided back to the house, leaving Diego baffled.

They're keeping secrets. Diego thought, getting the wheelbarrow. He looked over to see Freddy impossibly lifting another concrete planter, with Juan Carlos acting as if it was normal. *And Juan Carlos is in on it.*

He started filling the bed, mumbling under his breath the entire time. This wasn't how he wanted to spend his Saturday. He wanted to be off doing something with Alex, except Alex was at the local gym teaching kids interested in computers and computer programming. That sounded like heaven to Diego compared to this manual labor.

"Done," Diego announced, dumping the last bag into the bed. Wiping his brow with the back of his arm, he sighed.

Juan Carlos walked up with Freddy in tow. He gasped in horror. "Diego, what did you do?"

"I filled the stupid flower bed," Diego answered with a questioning look.

Juan Carlos made the sign of the cross. "Please, Lord, give me the strength not to smack this estupido."

"What?" Diego asked, perplexed.

Freddy shook his head. "Tío, you were supposed to mix the soil, not just dump it in."

"Well, we can mix it now," Diego said, not understanding the problem. "Grab a shovel and we'll mix it now."

Freddy shrugged. "Can't. It has to be mixed by hand, and I—"

"He has allergies." Juan Carlos finished quickly. "He's allergic to the plant that Esmerelda is going to plant there, so he can't touch it."

Diego stumbled over his thoughts, trying to understand the reasoning. "Wait. What? That's not how allergies work."

"Diego!" Esmerelda exclaimed, walking up. "What did you do?"

Diego put his hands up in a placating manner. "Guys, it's not that bad. We just have to mix the soil."

"Well, you had best get started if you want to be done before Alex gets here." Juan Carlos admonished.

"Freddy?" Diego questioned.

Juan Carlos huffed, irritated. "I told you he can't—"

"No." Diego cut him off. Pointing past Juan Carlos and Esmerelda, he said, "Freddy."

They turned to see what Diego was pointing at. Freddy was running away from them, toward the eastern side of the building. Diego sensed something was off with Freddy. He leaped into action, running past Juan Carlos and Esmerelda.

Running in front of Freddy, Diego blocked his path. "Freddy, are you okay?"

Freddy snarled at Diego, who found himself flying into bushes with a swipe of Freddy's hand. Diego pulled himself to his feet. He saw Esmerelda rushing past, then felt Juan Carlos's hands on him.

"Diego, are you okay? Is anything broken?" Juan Carlos asked, feeling his arm for injury.

Dazed, Diego blinked at Juan Carlos. He looked over at Freddy. He had reached the edge of the garden and was leaning over. Esmerelda was a few feet behind him. Alarmed, Diego shook Juan Carlos off.

"Esmeralda!" Diego shouted, running after Esmerelda. He ignored the shouts from Juan Carlos to stop. He couldn't. From the way Freddy knocked him aside, he knew Esmeralda wouldn't fare much better.

He reached Freddy just as Esmerelda did. "Freddy, what's wrong?" She asked, out of breath.

Freddy didn't take his eyes off the horizon. "Can't you hear it?" He spoke in a dreamy voice. "That song. It's calling me."

"Freddy, there's no song." Diego tried to pull Freddy from the edge, but he pushed Diego away.

Juan Carlos tugged at Diego's arm. "Diego, this is private family business."

"Diego, go, please," Esmerelda begged softly. "Freddy wouldn't want you to see him like this."

Diego reluctantly let Juan Carlos pull him away. "Come, I'll help you mix the soil."

CHAPTER 3

SMILING DOWN AT THE BEAUTIFUL naked young man lying on the blanket in the barn, Francisco slipped on his pants. Concern crept along the edges of his post-coitus bliss. What they had just done would land them both in prison, if not worse, if they were caught.

Picking up Sabastian's pants, Francisco tossed them at him. "Get dressed. Don Marcos could be back any minute."

Sabastian caught the pants with a yawn and a stretch. "He'll be gone all afternoon. He said he had business with some Gitana."

"We can't do this again," Francisco stated bluntly as he pulled on his shirt. "If anyone found out." Closing his eyes, Francisco shook his head at the thought. "This never happened, okay? This never happened."

Feeling Sabastian's delicate hands on his shoulders, Francisco opened his eyes. "But it did, and I never want to forget it."

"But you must, please, go," Francisco pleaded, with a breaking heart. "Go back to your fresh-baked breads, freshly cured meats, and sweet wines that flow like water. Forget about me, because I've already forgotten about you."

Sabastian pressed their foreheads together. "How could I ever forget about you? When from the first moment I saw you from my window, I knew you. How can I forget you when every day my soul sings out for you? You can't tell me it's not the same for you."

"It is," Francisco said softly. "But we can never be together. Even if I weren't some lowly farm-hand and you weren't the ward of the richest man in the province, they would never let us be together. Ese es nuestro triste peña."

Sabastian ran a hand over Francisco's stubbled cheek. "Then we'll run away to the new world. We'll hire on with a ship, and once we make port, we'll escape into the jungles and live out our lives together."

"Why do the dreams of lovers sound exactly like those of foolish men?" Francisco laughed bitterly. "You know I cannot leave my family. They need me. Elias needs me."

Sabastian pulled Francisco close. "I need you."

"Please, don't make it harder than it already is," Francisco said with heartache in his voice. Pulling away, he said, "Go. Go before we're caught."

Sabastian pulled Francisco back into his arms. "If I'm to leave and to never know your touch again, at least let me leave with the taste of you on my lips."

"Sabastian." A tear ran down Francisco's cheek.

Their lips brushed. Deepening the kiss, Francisco put his arms around Sabastian. Holding the man he loved but could never have in this life, was torture. His heart broke and mended a thousand times over. The words of hope he told Elias came back to him. *Maybe one day, people like us can live freely and openly.*

Neither of them knew their entire exchange had been heard by interloping ears. Lost in the kiss, they did not hear the barn door open or the footsteps that followed. The air around them began to chill and fill with the smell of death and decay. Breaking the kiss, Francisco and Sabastian saw the last person either of them wanted to see.

"Don Marcos, I can explain!" Francisco panicked, pushing Sabastian behind him. With a flick of his hand, Francisco was tossed to the side.

Sabastian pleaded, "Don Marcos, please, I love him!"

Francisco picked himself up. He looked at Don Marcos. He could not believe what he was seeing. Don Marcos's eyes glowed red with fire. Blackness billowed around him like a cape. The face of a young man in pain appeared before it was dragged back into the darkness.

"Love? What do I care of love?" Don Marcos's thunderous voice shook the rafters. "I hope it was worth it because you both shall now pay for your love."

Francisco heard the snarl and howls of the wild dogs circling the barn. "Please, Don Marcos, punish me. It was my fault. I seduced him," Francisco pleaded.

Francisco recoiled when Don Marcos cocked his head at him. This unholy creature resembled nothing of the distinguished gentleman that the men of the province envied. His honey-amber skin was gray and sallow. Paper thin, it draped loosely on the frame of the body that once made the women swoon.

"How dare you take what is mine?!" The barn shook with Don Marcos's anger. "Do you know how long it took me to find a pure angelic soul to feast upon?!" Francisco was hurdled across the barn into a beam. "One that was untouched and knew nothing of carnal desire!" Francisco's body collided with Sabastian's. "Perhaps the agony of your wretched souls will satiate the hunger inside me."

Sabastian cradled Francisco's bruised and battered body. "Our love can endure anything you can throw at us." Looking deep into Francisco's eyes, Sabastian kissed him. "Our souls are intertwined, destined to find one another in this and every other lifetime. You cannot break that bond."

"No, but I can stretch it so thin that it causes you nothing but pain." Don Marcos let out a malicious laugh. Francisco and Sabastian were flung against the barn wall. They were pinned by an invisible force, arms splayed out, fingers just shy of touching. "Imagine lifetime after lifetime, being so close but never touching!"

"I love you," Francisco said from the depths of his heart. "No matter what he does, I'll find you. I promise."

"The two of you shall never be together again." Wisps of gray smoke-like mist poured from Don Marcos's hands. It slithered around Sabastian and Francisco. "My foolish Sabastian, you wanted to head to the new world to escape me? Then that is where I shall send you and send your soul." Sabastian cried out in pain as the coiled grayness constricted around his body.

"Francisco," Don Marcos said with utter disgust in his voice. "You filthy mongrel. You wanted to sniff around and steal my scraps?" Francisco screamed in pain from the grayness squeezing itself into his body. "I shall use you to bind one of my captured mystical wolves that serves me. Your angst and sorrow over your lost love shall seep into him until he is broken."

Pain radiated through Francisco's body, but it was nothing compared to the pain of knowing he'd lose Sabastian forever. Screaming in agony, he desperately stretched his fingers out to reach Sabastian's. To his shock and delight, their fingertips brushed.

Don Marcos's expression of wicked delight morphed into that of incredulous horror. The pain ebbed away. A tiny speck of light blossomed in the void that surrounded Don Marcos. It grew larger and larger, with other specks appearing around it. The light burst forth and freed itself, causing Don Marcos to shriek out in pain.

Released from the mystical hold, Sabastian and Francisco fell to the floor. Feeling as if his body was being torn apart and reassembled, Francisco reached for Sabastian, only to have his hand pass through his love.

Don Marcos cried out again. Another burst of light freed itself. Francisco saw the face of a young man in it. Another burst of light; this time, he saw a young woman. Bursts of light with the faces of young men and women erupted from Don Marcos, sending the unearthly man stumbling back.

The lights swirled above them. Don Marcos reached up a hand to snatch them back. The door to the barn busted open. Standing there, to Francisco's surprise and dismay, stood Elias, poised to fight, with a hissing barn cat at their side.

CHAPTER 4

"IS FREDDY OKAY?" DIEGO ASKED, thrusting his arm into the soil. When no answer came, he looked over at Juan Carlos. He was on his hands and knees in the garden with Diego, hand-tilling the dirt. Diego asked again, "Is Freddy okay?"

Juan Carlos paused. He finally said, "He's okay. Can we please get this done? I have plans for tonight."

"If he's sick, maybe we can do something, maybe come up with some sort of treatment," Diego offered. Freddy and he were more than friendly rivals. They never said it out loud, but they were brothers, not by blood, but by love.

"Drop it, Diego. It's none of our business," Juan Carlos responded curtly.

Diego should have known by Juan Carlos's brisk tone to do just that, but he pressed on. "We could help him—"

"Drop it, Diego!" Diego was taken aback by the sharpness of Juan Carlos's tone. Juan Carlos took a deep breath. "I'm sorry. Some things we can't fix. If you want to help Federico, let's get this garden ready for planting."

Diego reluctantly dropped the subject. Hand-tilling the soil, he kept an eye on Freddy and Esmerelda. With an arm around Freddy, she guided him back inside the penthouse. Diego noticed Freddy looking back to the edge of the building where he had been standing.

That's no sickness. Diego eyed Juan Carlos digging into the dirt. *Something's going on and they're not telling me.*

"This should be good enough," Juan Carlos announced, standing and brushing the dirt off himself. "Come on, let's get cleaned up."

Diego stood. Eyeing Juan Carlos, he asked the one question he needed an answer to. "Is Freddy going to be okay?"

"He will be," Juan Carlos answered after a moment of thought. "Come on, let's get you cleaned up for Alex."

As they headed inside, Diego's stomach growled at the delicious smell of Esmerelda's cooking. Esmerelda swatted his hand when he tried to steal a piece of bacon. Laughing at him, Juan Carlos nudged Diego on to his room.

While showering off the day's labor, Diego's thoughts were consumed by Freddy. *What am I missing? What aren't they telling me?* Getting out of the shower and drying off, he made a decision. *I'm going to help Freddy whether they like it or not.*

Dressed in an old tee and gray sweatpants, he was happy to find Alex sitting at the kitchen island talking with Esmerelda. That happiness turned to annoyance when he caught sight of the strip of bacon Alex was nibbling on.

"Why does he get bacon, and I get my hand swatted?" Diego asked, coming up behind Alex and putting his arms around him.

"Because he has manners and asked nicely," Esmerelda playfully scolded.

Diego pecked Alex on the cheek, then slid onto the stool beside him. "I have manners."

"Really?" Esmerelda scoffed. "Does someone with manners complain about bacon or ask the man he's dating how his day was first?"

"In this house, bacon," Juan Carlos answered, coming up and putting a hand on Alex's shoulder. "How was your day? Was it a good turnout?"

Diego loved how Alex brightened when he started talking about the Saturday classes. "Twice as big as last week."

"Diego and I will have to double our weekly donation then, right, Diego?" Juan Carlos sat down on Alex's other side.

"Right. Wait. We're paying for the class?" Diego reached for a strip of bacon, only to have his hand swatted again. "Hey! I paid for that bacon!"

"Alex." Esmerelda looked at Diego but spoke to Alex. "What kind of tail would you like Diego to have?"

"Tail?" Puzzled, Alex turned to Diego. "What is she talking about? Are you, like, a furry?"

"No!" Diego exclaimed.

Alex put a gentle hand on Diego's knee. "It's okay if you're a furry. I won't judge. I bet you're something cute, like a bunny. Go and put your stuff on for us right now. We accept you."

"I'm not a furry." Diego stared at Alex in disbelief. "Esmerelda keeps threatening to give me a tail. Why would you think I'm a furry?"

"Because Esmerelda asked what type of tail I wanted for you. If you're not a furry," Alex paused in thought, "are you into puppy play?"

"No!" Diego gaped at Alex. "Wait, are you into puppy play?" Diego eyed Alex. "I can see it. I bet you make a cute puppy."

With his head in his hands, Juan Carlos groaned. "Esmeralda, would you please stop threatening to give Diego a tail?"

"Thank you!" Diego exclaimed.

Juan Carlos finished, "Just do it already."

"Exactly! Hey! Wait! No!" Diego's eyes grew wide. "Please, don't give me a tail! I'll have to alter all my pants!"

Alex chimed in, "Except for that pair with the zipper in the back or those leather chaps you wore—"

"Enough." Esmerelda shoved a piece of bacon into each of their mouths. "Juan Carlos told me about your joint ramblings." She shook her head. "But to experience it in person..."

Sitting down beside Diego, Freddy asked, "What are we talking about?"

"No!" Esmerelda quickly put more pieces of bacon into Diego's and Alex's mouths. "I'm not living through that again."

"How about we eat?" Juan Carlos suggested, picking up the plate of bacon and moving to the already-set table. "I do have plans this evening."

Everyone followed, sitting down at the round table. Diego saw Freddy pause, debating whether to take the open seat beside Alex or the one beside Juan Carlos. Juan Carlos wordlessly moved seats to take the spot beside Alex, letting Freddy take the seat beside Diego.

Scratching at his chest, Freddy asked, "So you and Diego are still together, huh?"

"You ask me that every time I see you." Alex laughed it off. "Yes. Why? Are you having regrets?"

Diego noticed that Freddy had stopped scratching his chest and was patting it lightly. Suspiciously he asked, "How's everything going, Freddy?"

"Freddy, can you help me bring the food to the table?" Esmerelda called from the kitchen.

Without answering Diego's question, Freddy got up from the table. Diego looked over to see Juan Carlos glaring at him. They would have words later. Very loud words with which Juan Carlos would speak and Diego listen.

"Eat up," Esmerelda said, setting two tortilla Españolas down on the table. She took the seat Freddy had vacated. "I have two more in the oven keeping warm, so don't hold back."

Taking the remaining seat, Freddy sat a plate of sausage links and patties down. "You know I won't."

"Um," Alex said, confused. "I thought you said we were having tortillas." He pointed to the potato and egg dish that Esmerelda was currently cutting into. "That doesn't look like any tortilla I've ever seen."

Juan Carlos cut a slice. "It's a tortilla Española," he explained, setting the slice on Alex's plate. "Try it. I'm sure you'll love it."

"It's normally served as a breakfast or brunch dish," Esmerelda explained, passing the tortilla to Freddy, away from Diego before he could get a slice. "Since Freddy and Juan Carlos have been begging me to make them one, I figured this would be the perfect time."

Alex took a bite. "This is good." He looked at Diego's empty plate. "Aren't you having any?"

"I would if people would stop moving the food away from me," Diego growled.

"I'm sorry, babe." Alex reached over and brought one of the tortillas over to Diego. He looked at everyone else and noticed the tension in the room. "Is something wrong?"

Esmerelda broke the tense silence. "No, nothing is wrong." She passed the plate of sausage over to Diego. "I think we've been picking on Diego too much today." She gave Diego a warm smile. "I'm sorry, Diego. I won't threaten to give you a tail anymore."

"Thank you." Diego returned the smile.

Not knowing what was going on, Alex turned his attention to Freddy. "Freddy, the owner of the gym said you're leaving the gym to focus on your art. What do you have planned?"

Diego saw the three conspirators stop eating. Uncomfortably, Freddy answered, "Yeah, and I've got the building to manage."

"Oh, yeah. You move in this coming week, right?" Diego watched Freddy shift nervously at Alex's question.

Freddy took a bite and chewed it slowly, biding time to answer the question. "Yeah, Monday, if all things go well."

"Why wouldn't things go well?" Alex asked, curiously.

Freddy shrugged. "You know, shit happens."

"Esmerelda, what do you have planned for tonight?" Juan Carlos asked, strategically changing the subject.

"I'm going to a charity auction." Diego noticed that she looked at Freddy when she spoke. "I have reason to believe a lost family heirloom is up for auction."

Diego covertly watched everyone. He took a bite to keep from showing his smile when Alex asked, "What is it? How was it lost?"

"It's a jewel, of sorts. Costume jewelry, really." Diego heard the hint of half-truth in Esmerelda's words. "It changed our family's destiny, then disappeared."

Freddy chuffed in derision. "It's probably another false lead. I've given up hope of finding it centuries ago."

"You must not give up hope, primo." Esmerelda put a hand on Freddy's. "You heard the..." Esmerelda self-corrected mid-sentence, "...the call earlier."

"If it's not the right one, maybe I can search for it for you," Alex commented, trying to be helpful.

Seeing that Freddy was getting visibly upset over the conversation, Diego decided to change the subject again. "Freddy, isn't your birthday coming up? Do you have anything big planned?"

"Nope," Freddy answered gruffly. "I'm going camping."

Seeing he was getting nowhere with Freddy, Diego addressed Juan Carlos. "So when do I get to meet this man of yours? You've been out on like twelve dates with him, and I've yet to meet him."

"If possible, you'll never meet him." Juan Carlos answered smoothly. "I don't want you scaring him away." Juan Carlos narrowed his eyes at Diego. "How did you know I had a date tonight?"

Diego acted innocent. "You told me you were going out. I just assumed it was a date."

"That reminds me, where are we going tonight?" Alex stepped in, trying to deflect Juan Carlos's wrath. "I need to know how to dress."

Thankful, Diego squeezed Alex's knee under the table. "Wear your new blue shirt and black slacks with your new shoes."

"I don't have a new blue shirt, black slacks, and shoes." Alex cocked his head at Diego. "Did you buy me new clothes? Again?"

Diego swallowed hard before answering nervously, "No."

"I told you to stop buying me things." Alex huffed. He turned to Juan Carlos. "He never listens. He just does what he wants."

Juan Carlos shrugged. "Just be glad you're one of the things he wants to do."

"This is the weirdest family conversation ever." Freddy laughed, going for seconds.

Esmerelda laughed. "This is the weirdest family ever."

CHAPTER 5

E LIAS PAUSED TO CATCH THEIR breath at the gate to the hacienda. Felix was at their side, poised to strike. Above, dark clouds had moved in to blot out the sun. The smell of doom and death lingered in the air. The sound of the snapping and growling wild dogs drew Elias's attention to the barn.

It was the first time Elias had seen the ungodly beasts, with their coats as black as midnight. They lurked around the barn, hackles raised, awaiting the command to attack. One of them must have caught their scent, because it turned its head with a snarl to fix its blood-red eyes on Elias and Felix.

Fear gripped Elias. Without thinking, they touched the medallion around their neck. Elias felt a warm light embracing them like a warm hug. They had a sense that they were not alone. They could feel others in the light with them. It did not quell the fear, but it gave Elias the strength to face it.

Serenity came over Elias when they heard the voice of the Gitana in their head. <You are braver than you know. We will help guide you, sister. Draw your dagger and cast these demon dogs back into Hell.>

The wild dogs had gathered in a pack formation, teeth bared at Elias and Felix. The beasts snarled. Felix hissed back. Elias pulled out the Gitano dagger. They could feel those in the light guiding their movements.

The beasts charged them. Elias and Felix ran to meet the attack. The first beast snapped its jaws at Elias as it lunged at them. Elias spun with the grace of a Flamenco dancer, dragging the dagger along the creature's side. The bastardized animal cried out in anger.

Black blood oozed from the creature. It staggered before collapsing onto its side, snapping its teeth at Elias. It promised revenge with a pitiful growl before melting into the ground. It faded away, banished back to the depths of Hell from which it came, leaving no trace that it had ever once existed here.

Elias saw Felix on the back of one of the monstrous creatures, digging his claws into it. Black blood leaked from the beast where Felix tore at its skin. The demon dog turned its head to snap at Felix, but the ferocious feline was out of reach. Felix leaped from the creature as it stumbled and fell over, releasing a mournful cry for vengeance before it, too, was gone.

Elias moved with the grace of a dancer and the skill of an assassin. Felix pounced from beast to beast, tearing into their flesh. One by one, they dispatched the Hellish hounds back into the darkness until only one remained—the largest and most fearsome.

The hulking beast stood in front of the barn, blocking their path. Snarling with hackles raised and fangs bared, the demon dog attacked. Felix moved to meet the beast, only to be swatted away like a pesky fly by one of its massive paws. It drew closer to Elias. They stood their ground.

The beast jumped. Elias raised their hand. The demon beast froze in the air, the tip of its nose pressed into Elias's palm. Elias could smell the foul stench of the damned creature's breath and saw the surprise in its crazed red eyes. Elias pushed against its muzzle.

The Hell hound's body cracked with lines of white light. The cracks grew wider. The light grew brighter. Then the beast exploded, leaving only a small ball of white light in Elias's hand.

They hurled the orb at the barn. It collided with the barn door, causing the wood to shatter and splinter in a cloud of smoke.

With Felix by their side, Elias rushed to the barn. They stood there, not understanding what they were seeing. Francisco and Sabastian were on the ground. Francisco's body was twisting in ways a body shouldn't, while Sabastian's seemed to be fading. Standing in Elias's path to the two men with swirling white light above him was the fiend that Elias knew was the demon, Don Marcos.

"I thought I ended your line when I ambushed that foolish Gitana," Don Marcos hissed at Elias.

Elias didn't know where the pride and determination in their words came from when they said, "There will always be a Gitana."

"What have you done with my demon dogs?" Don Marcos pointed a boney finger at Elias. "No matter, I can trap more low-level demons to bind with poor, unfortunate souls."

With the dagger in hand, Elias stood poised to strike. "Not before we send you back to Hell."

"Foolish boy. You are no match for me." Gray flames engulfed Don Marcos's skeletal hand. A sphere shot forth at Elias and Felix.

Evading the blast of magic, Elias jumped left, Felix to the right. "I'm not a boy." Saying the words out loud and finally accepting their truth lifted a heavy burden that Elias did not know they were carrying. An overwhelming sense of love flowed into Elias.

<We love and accept you, Elias.> The Gitana spoke in their mind. <Feel the strength and power of your truth. Embrace it. Use it. For you are the Gitana.>

"I will feast on your soul!" Don Marcos shot another magical gray orb that Elias dodged. "Then I will devour the souls of everyone you love!"

Elias hid behind one of the barn's beams. Gray orbs flew by. Elias noticed they were getting smaller and slower. *What should I do?* Elias clutched the medallion in one hand and held the dagger, ready to strike in the other. *Someone help me, please.*

"Meow," Felix called from behind stacks of hay. Elias saw he had dragged a satchel with him. It was the salt satchel Francisco used to cure small amounts of meat. "Meow," Felix repeated more urgently.

<Take the salt,> the Gitana ordered Elias.

Knowing she would not steer them wrong, Elias nodded at Felix. The tenacious tabby ran out to distract Don Marcos. Elias dove behind the bales, snatching up the leather satchel with the precious crystals. They looked at Felix, expertly dodging the weakening blasts from Don Marcos.

"Die puss! Die!" Don Marcos raged, shooting blast after blast at Felix.

Elias dipped their hand into the satchel and pulled out a handful of salt. <What do I do with this?>

<Cast it upon Don Marcos and trap him,> the Gitana answered.

The salt pulsed with light in Elias's hand. They watched Don Marcos for the right moment. He turned away from Elias to strike out again at Felix. Elias moved from behind the bale and toward Don Marcos. Elias threw the salt at the demon. It scattered in the air, pelting Don Marcos and burned into his skin.

Don Marcos screamed in agony. The medallion the Gitana gave Elias glowed around her neck. They knew what they needed to do. Elias put their hand into the bag that carried Francisco's lunch. Elias pulled out the small jar of honey for the bread. It glowed brightly in their hand. They opened the jar.

The glowing honey flowed out of the jar to wrap around Don Marcos. Don Marcos flailed about, trying to free himself while the glowing amber engulfed his body. Elias extended their open hand toward Don Marcos. Closing their hand, the swirling honey, with Don Marcos inside, constricted down into a small round orb.

Elias breathed a sigh of relief; then they panicked when they looked over at Francisco and Sabastian. Francisco's clothes were shredded, and hair was starting to spout all over his body. Sabastian was a shadow of who he was. Elias rushed over to them, and the honey orb dropped to the ground.

"Francisco!" Elias cried out, reaching their cousin's side in a panic. "I can fix this. I can save you!"

<I wish you could, my sister,> the Gitana said. <You are not powerful enough to break Don Marco's curse.>

Tears fell down Elias's face. "Please! Someone help me!"

"Meow," Felix said mournfully.

Elias didn't feel as much as sense the hands that touched their shoulders. Two of the souls from the swirling light had come down. They had the form of a man and of a woman. They looked at Elias and then at the rapidly changing Francisco and fading Sabastian.

Speaking together in Elias's mind, they said, <We cannot break the curse, but we can help you alter it.>

Elias put their hands out, one toward Francisco and the other toward Sabastian. "With the strength of hope and love in our hearts, this curse shall one day be broken when these two are reunited." Francisco and Sabastian began to glow. Elias felt their love and felt the beast trying to tear itself out of Francisco.

Elias looked at Sabastian. "One day, you and my cousin will find one another again. It will be many lifetimes, and I am sorry for that. Sing for him, and one day he will come. Keep his love in your heart." Sabastian faded away.

"I'm sorry, Francisco." Elias held both hands toward his cousin. "I will spend as many lifetimes as it takes to reunite the two of you." Elias drew on their love for their cousin. "I cannot expel the beast in you, but maybe I can help you reason with it." Francisco cried out in pain as his body snapped back to normal.

"It doesn't want to be in you," Elias said through clenched teeth. "Hear me, creature of the moon, help my cousin find his love, and we can free you of his mortal confines."

Francisco threw back his head and let out a howl. The hair retreated. His body returned to normal. Naked, he collapsed onto the ground. Elias, exhausted, lifted their cousin into their arms. Felix joined them, looking curiously at the wolf that was etched into Francisco's skin.

Elias ran a hand over the tattoo. "Thank you," they told it. Elias looked to the souls that had helped them. "Thank you, as well." They nodded, joined the rest, and flowed up through the ceiling.

Elias looked to where Felix was hissing. A beady-eyed rat stood on its hind legs and its tail slapping about in the hole where the door was. In its mouth, it held the honey orb that held Don Marcos's demon soul. It twitched its whiskers, then ran off with Felix chasing after it.

<Don Marcos's minion has already escaped into one of its many bolt tunnels,> the Gitana told Elias solemnly. <You must find him and expel him to Hell before he finds a way to break free.>

<I'm sorry,> Elias told her. <I should have grabbed the orb.>

Elias felt her warm embrace. <It's not your fault. I would have done the same.>

"Elias," Francisco called out weakly. "Where is Sabastian?"

Elias stroked their cousin's hair. "I don't know, but we'll find him. We'll find him."

CHAPTER 6

JUAN CARLOS GLIDED THROUGH the tables of his favorite restaurant to where his date, Aaron, sat waiting. Juan Carlos couldn't help but smile when the dapper man spotted him and stood. Embracing the man in a casual hug and placing a friendly peck on the cheek, Juan Carlos forgot about the day's annoyances.

"Hello, Aaron." Juan Carlos gave the man a causal once over. "My, don't you look handsome tonight."

Returning the peck on Juan Carlos's cheek, Aaron teased, "Just tonight?" Pulling out the chair for Juan Carlos, he added, "You look as ravishing as ever."

"Thank you." Sitting down, Juan Carlos smiled shyly. "How on earth did you manage to get my favorite table at my favorite restaurant?"

Taking his seat, Aaron gave Juan Carlos a puzzled look. "I didn't. You did."

"Why are there four place settings?" Juan Carlos asked, a twinge of fear in his voice. He quickly stood up. "We need to go. We'll have dinner somewhere else; grab something from a drive-thru."

"Too late." Aaron pointed behind Juan Carlos. "Diego is here."

Juan Carlos turned around in horror to see Diego and Alex coming toward them. "You're about to see why I wouldn't let you pick me up at my place."

"It can't be as bad as you say." Aaron laughed.

"No." Juan Carlos turned back to Aaron. "It's much worse."

Juan Carlos turned back just in time to receive Diego's embrace. "Juan Carlos! Funny running into you here," Diego said with mock surprise. Moving toward Aaron, he extended his hand and said, "This must be the elusive Detective Aaron Heath. Diego Sanz."

"Call me Aaron, please." Aaron stood and took Diego's hand. "Pleasure to finally meet you."

Alex not so subtly knocked Diego aside. Taking Aaron's hand, he said, "Alex Freeman. This ambush was not my idea, and I had nothing to do with it. Please, don't arrest me for whatever happens tonight."

"Are you expecting more people to join you?" Diego asked innocently as he motioned to the table settings.

Groaning, Juan Carlos sat down. "Diego, sit down. We know you orchestrated this. We might as well get it over with."

"Well, if you insist." Diego smiled, starting to sit down. "Ouch!" Diego cried out when Juan Carlos smacked him.

"Be a gentleman and pull your date's seat out for them." Juan Carlos politely reprimanded him.

Alex chuckled softly when he sat down in the chair Diego pulled out for him. "Thank you, Diego."

"So, Detective Heath," Diego said, returning to his seat, "are you going to be my daddy?"

Aaron's eyes bulged. "Excuse me?"

"Diego!" Juan Carlos exclaimed.

Alex put his head in his hands. "This is going to turn out so badly."

"He does mean like a father figure, right?" Aaron asked uncomfortably. "He doesn't mean like a 'daddy,' daddy? Does he?"

With his hands still on his head, Alex groaned. "I sure hope not."

"Aaron, you brought your sidearm, didn't you?" Juan Carlos asked, seething.

Confused, Aaron turned his attention to Juan Carlos. "Yes."

"Would you be a dear and shoot Diego?" Juan Carlos asked.

Alex lifted his head from his hand. "Please, don't shoot him before our date is over."

Stunned, Aaron said, "I'm not shooting him."

"Then hand me your gun, and I'll shoot him." Juan Carlos thrust his hand at Aaron.

Diego glared at Juan Carlos. "You said you wouldn't shoot me again."

"Again?" Alex and Aaron blurted out at the same time.

Juan Carlos waved his hand around dismissively. "He pissed me off, and we needed to test something."

"You said it was an accident!" Diego stood suddenly, knocking into a passing server carrying a tray of food, sending them crashing into a neighboring table. "I'm so sorry!"

"Now you see why I didn't want you to meet him." Juan Carlos sighed. "You should have let me shoot him."

"Oh, I think this is going to be a very interesting dinner." Aaron laughed, watching Diego help the server up.

Wide-eyed, Alex yelled, "Diego! Stop brushing food off that server's crotch!"

"Gentlemen." The maître d' came up to the table. "Is there a problem here?"

Juan Carlos sighed. "No, just Diego being Diego. Please, add those tables' bills to our own, the server's dry-cleaning bill, and..." Juan Carlos did his best to control his temper. "Diego, would you please stop brushing that poor server's crotch and sit your ass down?"

"I'm so sorry," Diego told the maître d'. "It won't happen again."

Alex groaned, "It probably will."

"I'll alert the wait staff," the maître d' said, rolling his eyes and walking away.

The table was quiet for a moment before Diego broke the silence right as the server arrived at the table. "So, Aaron, you never answered whether you're going to be my daddy or not."

"I, um, can come back," the server said uncomfortably.

Wide-eyed, Alex exclaimed, "Diego!"

"What?" Diego asked, confused.

"He does mean like a father figure, right?" Aaron asked Juan Carlos. "Please, tell me he means like a father figure."

"I sure hope so." Juan Carlos looked to the distraught server. "I'm going to need a bottle of red wine."

"For the table?" The server asked.

Glaring at Diego, Juan Carlos said, "For me."

"Diego and I will have water," Alex spoke up.

Aaron looked at Diego, then Juan Carlos. "Triple whisky on the rocks."

"He's not coming back, is he?" Alex asked.

Juan Carlos exhaled. "He will. He gets hazard pay."

"Anyways!" Diego huffed. "Aaron, are you—"

"Diego, I swear if you ask that one more time, I'm going to stab you with my shrimp fork," Juan Carlos threatened.

Alex shook his head. "You'll get used to it, or so I'm told."

"Well, to answer Diego's question," Aaron cleared his throat nervously, "or at least the question I hope he is asking, Juan Carlos and I have just started dating. Who knows where our relationship is going, but I do have genuine feelings for your father."

"Diego is not my son," Juan Carlos corrected.

Diego added, "He's my mamacita."

Seeing the confusion building at the table, Alex decided to explain. "Juan Carlos took Diego in and raised him. When Diego turned eighteen, he had his last name legally changed to Sanz. It was a big ordeal; he ended up on the news." Alex saw Diego and Juan Carlos staring at him. "What? Someone sent me a link to the video."

"Your drinks." The server said, setting the glasses around the table before presenting Juan Carlos with his bottle. "Your wine. I was told this is your favorite."

Diego suddenly blurted out, "Wait! Did he think?"

"And we have realization." Alex announced.

Putting a hand on Diego's knee, Juan Carlos said, "If you value your life, you will be quiet and not mention this ever again." Juan Carlos returned his attention to the server. "For the sake of time and everyone's sanity, I'll order for the table."

With their orders placed, the nervous server rushed away. Everyone was silent, watching Juan Carlos. Juan Carlos swirled the wine in his glass before taking a healthy drink. Setting the empty glass down, he poured himself another. "What? I'm not going to make a scene here." Juan Carlos turned his steely gaze to Diego. "I'll do it in private, where no one can hear his screams."

"Aaron," Alex spoke up. "Have you guys made any progress in finding Jimmy?"

Relieved by the change of subject, Aaron said, "None. The trail went cold about a hundred meters into the woods from where we found his truck."

"Of course, Mayor Trainer and his lapdog, Police Chief Brutus, are putting a real effort into finding him." Juan Carlos scoffed. "I'm glad we cut all our political donations to them."

Diego perked up. "We did?"

"Yes, dear." Juan Carlos sipped his wine. "It's in the memo I didn't send you last week."

"That solution you gave us to dissolve that gunk Timmy and Dr. Wyatt were trapped in worked like a charm," Aaron jumped in, cutting Diego off.

Juan Carlos motioned to Alex. "Thank Alex, here. He's the one that found the base formula in our database."

"I just found the formula." Alex blushed, still unaccustomed to praise. "Diego actually came up with the solution to dissolve it."

Smiling, Diego leaned forward to look at Alex. "Which I couldn't have done so quickly had you not found the formula."

"Maybe we should work together more often," Alex said, leaning and smiling back at Diego.

Seeing Aaron had downed most of his drink, Juan Carlos decided to steer the conversation elsewhere. "Aaron, I've been meaning to ask, I have an event in two weeks if you're free to be my escort."

"For Freddy's birthday?" Diego asked hopefully.

Juan Carlos continued, ignoring Diego, "It's for a fundraiser for Tio Pepe's House. I'm performing."

"You're bringing back Dolores Savaje?" Diego asked excitedly.

Trying to maintain his composure, Juan Carlos continued, "Do you think you can attend or—."

"Wait," Diego interrupted, looking at his phone. "That event is on Freddy's birthday. Are we seriously not doing anything for his birthday?"

"Diego," Alex whisper-shouted. "Will you let Juan Carlos ask Aaron out?"

Aaron reached across the table and took Juan Carlos's hand. "I'd be happy to escort you as Juan Carlos or as Dolores Savaje."

"Okay, now what about Freddy's birthday?" Diego asked tersely. "We've never not celebrated a birthday."

Juan Carlos closed his eyes. "Diego, can we talk about that later?"

"Okay," Diego grumbled after seeing the pleading in Alex's eyes. *And I'll be getting the truth out of him.*

CHAPTER 7

L EAVING THE AUCTION HALL, Esmerelda scanned the crowd, looking for the two men who had outbid her on the one item she had come here for. She was so close. In every lifetime, she was always close, but never this close. Don Marcos's prison was always slipping through her hands. She couldn't let it this time.

She spotted them, the plump man and the rat-faced, skinny boy. The man was frowning disap-provingly at the boy. The boy, ignoring the man, was busy typing away on his phone. The two were obviously squabbling quietly over something. Hopefully, it was about the honey amber orb and they'd welcome Esmerelda's offer to take away the object of their discontent.

Esmerelda maneuvered through the people with a skill only learned from spending your early twenties in crowded gay bars. She stood out in the sea of people dressed in their muted, dull blacks and grays in her navy-blue Flamenco-style dress with white dots and red ruffles at the bottom. She never understood why people could be so afraid of color or flair in their clothing.

Coming upon the two men, Esmerelda extended her hand in greeting. "Gentlemen, I'm Esmeralda Cesar Romero." She withdrew her hand when she saw the contempt in their eyes. Clearing her throat and straightening her shoulders, she asked, "I was wondering if I could implore you to sell me the orb you won in the auction. It is a lost family heirloom, and I'd very much like to have it back."

The plump man bristled. Speaking with condescension in his voice, he said, "Young lady, we are not in the business of buying things just to give them to," he looked her up and down, "those less fortunate."

"I'm sorry, you must have misheard me. I was offering to buy it off you," Esmeralda reiterated, trying to keep the politeness in her tone.

"Like you could pay what we did for the bobble. If you could, you would have outbid my son," the man scoffed.

Keeping her tone polite and friendly, Esmerelda continued, "No, I do not have the funds at the moment, but I have means of getting them."

"We do not want your whore or drug money," the plump man sneered.

The lights flickered with Esmerelda's quelled anger. "Sir, I assure you that my money is as clean as your white cotton briefs were before you soiled them by putting them on."

The plump man's face grew red with anger, but the rat-faced boy laughed. Putting his phone away and looking at Esmerelda, his thin lips stretched into a cold smile. "I'll sell it to you. For double what I paid."

"Fine." Esmerelda forced herself to continue smiling pleasantly.

The boy's grin stretched wider, making him look more rat-like. "Triple."

"Fine," Esmerelda said through clenched teeth.

Rat boy made a show of thinking it over. "Hhmm. On second thought, I'm not going to sell it. I think it'll make a pretty paperweight."

"Thank you for your time." Ignoring the laughs of the two men, Esmerelda nodded gracefully. *I wonder if I could turn the little brat into an actual rat.*

The rat-faced boy turned away from Esmerelda and toward his father. "Let's go. This place is boring. I want to hit the clubs tonight."

"When will you grow up, Finn?" The plump man groaned, putting a hand on the boy's shoulder and turning him away from Esmerelda.

Esmerelda watched as the two men pushed their way through the people toward the treasurer's office. Fighting the urge to use her powers, she turned back into the crowd. She would figure out other ways to get the orb. Freddy wouldn't like her plan, but desperate times called for desperate measures. She would not be robbed of this chance to break the curse.

She stepped out into the cool night air of Morgan City. She handed the valet her ticket. She thought about calling Juan Carlos but decided against it. He was on a date. A date with a cop. With what she was planning, it was best that he didn't know.

After slipping the valet a hundred-dollar bill, she got into her slick sports car. She carefully pulled out into the traffic of Morgan City. She was contemplating her next course of action and the possible legal ramifications when an incoming call came across her car's screen.

She immediately answered when she saw it was Juan Carlos. "Hola, caracola. Don't tell me your date is over already. It's only ten."

"Your place is magnificent, and that garden," Aaron commented. Juan Carlos had given him the grand tour, and now they were enjoying an after-dinner coffee together on the sofa.

"Thank you, and thank you for not running away in terror during dinner," Juan Carlos mused. "Diego can be a bit, err, much when it comes to the happiness of others."

Aaron laughed. "Why did he think it was okay to ask me if I was going to be his daddy?"

"He's a genius, business and technology-wise. Socially, well, you saw." Juan Carlos scooted over closer to Aaron. "Enough about Diego. Let's talk about us. Are you going to be my daddy?"

Aaron put an arm around Juan Carlos. Pulling him closer, he asked, "Why didn't you tell me you were bringing Dolores Savaje back?"

Juan Carlos pulled back to look at Aaron. "You knew I was Dolores Savaje?"

"I'm a detective." Aaron tugged Juan Carlos closer. "Plus, I used to go see you perform."

"You did not." Juan Carlos leaned back into Aaron.

"I did. You were my favorite performer. I tried to make every one of your performances. Why did you stop?" Aaron asked, shifting so Juan Carlos could rest against his chest.

Juan Carlos settled into Aaron. It wasn't something he liked to talk about. It was an ugly truth. Juan Carlos answered with a sigh. "When Diego was starting out, he wanted me there with him. Every meeting. He didn't see it, but I did. They weren't taking him seriously because he was a kid, and I was a flamboyant drag queen."

Juan Carlos drew comfort from Aaron hugging him close. "I had a decision to make. Let Diego's dreams die or do what I could to make them come true. I exchanged one form of drag for another and became the fiercest businessman the world had ever seen."

"Well, I'm glad that you're reviving her. I can't wait to see you out on that stage again." Aaron kissed the top of Juan Carlos's shaved head. "You've helped Diego fulfill his dream, and now you can live out yours, right?"

Juan Carlos ran a hand over Aaron's. "I've always loved performing. It was never my dream, though. I come from a time where you only dreamed of surviving and getting out, maybe having a husband and big family."

Aaron interlaced his fingers with Juan Carlos's. "Well, you did survive, and you did get out. I guess Diego is the start of a big family."

"Don't remind me." Juan Carlos laughed.

They settled into a comfortable silence. Juan Carlos rolled over and kissed Aaron. Deepening the kiss, they shifted on the sofa with Juan Carlos on top of Aaron. Juan Carlos was grateful that Diego had decided to spend the night at Alex's after he had told Diego, too. Aaron pulled him close.

"Really?" Juan Carlos groaned, hearing his phone ringing.

Laughing, Aaron asked, "What is that?"

"Diego, calling me," Juan Carlos griped, moving off Aaron.

Aaron sat up. "Is that?"

"Yes. Diego programmed it into my phone, and I can't change it." Juan Carlos snatched his phone off the end table.

"That's too funny. Let it play. I love 'Barbie Girl.'" Aaron snickered.

Trying not to be amused at Aaron laughing, Juan Carlos answered the phone. "This had better be good."

Diego pulled into the one empty spot near Alex's building. Dinner was a success, of sorts. He finally got to meet Aaron, though he had to trick both Juan Carlos and Aaron, and he had to promise the restaurant in writing he'd never come back.

"We're here," Diego announced to an unusually quiet Alex. Turning off the car, he asked, "Is something wrong?"

Exhaling loudly, Alex said, "Diego, Juan Carlos wasn't ready for you to meet Aaron, and you ambushed their date."

"Correction," Diego defended. "I orchestrated a date for me to meet him."

Alex's eyes grew wide. "That's even worse!"

Diego reached over and took Alex's hand. "I don't think you understand. I owe everything to Juan Carlos. If cyberstalking, doing background checks, and blackmailing Dion into helping arrange the date is wrong, then I'm going to be wrong."

"Please, tell me you didn't," Alex pleaded.

Diego grinned. "No, I just blackmailed Dion. Juan Carlos would have already done all that other stuff."

"Diego," Alex said calmly. "I get what Juan Carlos is to you, but didn't you think there was a reason Juan Carlos didn't want you to meet him yet?"

Diego shrugged. "Because we're still in litigation from when I went to check out the girl Dion was interested in?"

"Exactly." Alex paused. "Wait. What?"

Opening his door, Diego asked, "Can we continue this conversation upstairs in your apartment with fewer clothes on?"

"Fine, but the clothes stay on until we're done talking," Alex grumbled, getting out of the car.

Locking the car and taking Alex's hand, Diego mischievously said, "We'll see about that."

Alex side-bumped into Diego. "You're also going to tell me why Freddy not having a birthday party is upsetting you so much."

"When I went to live with Juan Carlos, I felt like a guest in his home. It wasn't until Freddy's birthday, a few weeks later, that I felt like I was part of the family." Diego's voice went somber. "Freddy had just blown out the candles, and I had faded away into a corner."

Diego choked up with emotion. "Freddy came over with a piece of cake and asked, 'Do you know what I wished for?' Before I could answer, he put his arm around me and said, 'Nothing. A brother is all I ever wanted, and now I have you.'"

"Oh, Diego." Alex pulled Diego into a hug.

Diego continued, "Then he smashed the cake into my face."

"Sounds about right." Alex laughed.

Hearing an angry growl, Diego moved Alex behind him. "What was that?"

"It's just a dog. We probably just spooked it." Alex turned to see two glowing yellow eyes. "Or, maybe it's something that's going to tear us limb from limb."

Diego turned around to see the eyes rise to human level. He shoved Alex behind him. "Stay behind me. If you get a chance, make a break for the car." A brown-clawed paw stepped into the light. "What is it?"

Both Diego and Alex stared wide-eyed at the creature that stepped forth out of the darkness. It had short brown fur all over its body. It stood hunched over on two canine legs with human-like hands. Its fingers ended in razor-sharp black nails. The wolf-like face snarled and snapped at them with long, sharp teeth.

"Is that a werewolf?" Alex asked, trying to mask the fear in his voice.

The creature snapped at Alex. Diego maneuvered himself to block the creature's view of Alex. "I don't know." The creature sniffed the air, then growled at Diego. "Back off, mutt." It bared its fangs at Diego.

"I don't think it likes being called 'mutt.'" Alex said, cowering when the creature snapped at him.

"I don't care." Diego pulled his keys out and unlocked his car. "I'll distract it while you get to the car."

"Are you crazy?! You don't have your suit! It'll tear you to pieces!" Alex argued.

Without thinking, Diego responded, "It's in the car. Now go!"

Alex cautiously took a step from behind Diego, only to jump back when the creature lunged toward him. Diego quickly moved between them, and the creature backed off. Diego motioned for Alex to move again. He did, and the creature lunged at him again. When Diego moved between them, the creature backed off again.

"Grab me by the waist and use me as a human shield," Diego ordered.

Alex argued, "I'm not doing that!"

"It's not after me. It's after you for some reason," Diego explained impatiently. "I don't know what you did to piss it off, but it won't attack you if I'm between you two."

Alex put his hands on Diego's hips. "You'd better be right." Keeping Diego between him and the canine creature, Alex moved them toward the car. "I can't believe this is working."

"When we get to the car, jump in. I'll be right behind you," Diego ordered. "Don't hesitate."

"Get ready. I'm opening the door," Alex announced.

Diego dodged a swipe. "Hurry, I don't think it cares if it hurts me anymore."

Alex slipped in the door, pulling Diego back along with him. Diego kicked out his feet together, catching the creature in its muzzle and sending it hurtling back. Diego sat up quickly and yanked the door shut right as the creature attacked again. The creature slammed into the glass, sending spider web cracks across the window.

The creature reared up and brought its paw back to slice its nails across the car. "No, you don't." Diego sneered, pressing a tiny blue button on the dash. The car shook slightly as blackness surrounded the vehicle. Red emergency lights lit on the dash and along the frame of the car. "That should keep him out."

"What the Hell is that thing, and why does it want me?" Alex asked, untangling himself and moving over to the passenger seat. The car rocked from the creature slamming into it.

They heard the scrape of claws against the tiny microbots that covered the car. Diego tapped away at the car's display screen. "I don't know. Fuck! The car won't start." The car jolted again, and then came the scrape of claws across the metal.

"What about your suit?" Alex asked in a panic.

Diego cocked his head at Alex. "How do you know about my suit?"

"Diego, this is not the time!" Alex shouted. "Focus, there's a dog monster trying to kill us."

Diego tapped on the screen. An error message popped up. Diego cleared the message and tried again. "Okay, all power is being diverted to protect the car. I'd have to drop the microbot armor and hope there's enough power to start the car."

"Can we call for help?" Alex asked.

Diego tapped away on the screen. "When the suit forms around you, tap your left temple. It's a direct line to Juan Carlos. If the car's armor fails, you'll be safe in the suit."

"What do you mean when the suit forms around me?" Alex's question was answered when the tiny microbots flowed out of a tiny compartment in the dash and enveloped him in the Shadow Guardian garb.

The car jolted again, nearly turning on its side. Diego repeated his instruction. "Tap your temple. I'm going to try and see if I can boost the power."

Alex tapped his temple. He heard a phone ringing. *Come on, Juan Carlos. Pick up.* He quietly cheered when Juan Carlos came on the line.

"This had better be good." Juan Carlos snapped.

Alex took a deep breath and blurted out, "It's Alex. Diego and I are trapped in the car by some crazed werewolf wolf thing. The microbot armor can't take much more. I think Diego is going to do something crazy because he put his suit on me."

"Tell Diego to stay in the car. I'm calling for help now." Juan Carlos said calmly. "I'm on my way."

The line went dead. Alex reached out to take Diego's hand. "He said he's sending help and to stay put." The car jolted again, then came the rapid-fire scrape of nails on metal.

"I've got to do something," Diego growled.

The scratching stopped. They heard the creature howl. They waited for the beast to crash into the car again, but nothing happened. Diego gave Alex's hand a squeeze. Diego pressed the button on the dash, commanding the microbot armor to withdraw.

"It's gone," Diego said, breathing a sigh of relief. He tapped on the screen, sending the Shadow Guardian microbots back into the console. "Let's see if we can find any clues as to what that was or what you did to piss it off."

Opening his door, Alex grumbled, "I didn't do anything to piss it off."

"Well, your armor held up. It's the car that needs to be redesigned for impact. We'll work on that on Monday," Diego commented, examining the car that was now in the middle of the road.

Alex shook his head in disbelief at Diego. "You're talking about work? Now?"

Looking around the ground for any bit of fur or stray hair, Diego countered, "We could talk about how long you've known I'm Shadow Guardian."

Alex was rescued from answering by the sound of the squealing brakes of a sedan with flashing blue lights. The vehicle had barely stopped before Juan Carlos ejected himself from the passenger's seat and came running toward them.

"Aye, mi niño!" Juan Carlos made a show of running to Alex and putting his arms around him. In his ear, Juan Carlos softly ordered, "You're too distraught to talk about it, and it happened so fast."

Aaron came trotting up. "Is everyone okay?"

Diego exchanged a look with Juan Carlos before answering, "Yeah, luckily, the prototype armor held up, but it still needs work."

"Alex, what do you remember?" Aaron asked, sensing Diego's deflection.

"We were walking, then this thing came running after us," Alex began to blubber. "Next thing I knew, Diego was throwing me in the car, then the window almost broke, then it was gone." Alex buried his face into Juan Carlos. "I just want to forget this night ever happened."

Patting Alex's back, Juan Carlos whispered, "Good boy."

"If I wasn't the only cop that would come out here, maybe we could have caught that beast," Aaron griped.

Esmerelda's sports car came racing around the corner, stopping millimeters from Aaron's sedan. She came flying out of the car. "Where's Freddy?"

"Freddy? Did you guys call Freddy, too?" Diego questioned.

Juan Carlos quickly answered, "I think he chased the creature off."

Diego caught the look Esmerelda and Juan Carlos shared. He decided to take a gamble. "Yeah, we should go looking for him."

"No, I'll look for him. I'm sure he's okay. You guys go home and get some rest." Esmeralda turned, the bottom of her dress whipping around when she did. They all turned to the sound of a howl in the distance. The sound was replaced by the sound of Esmerelda's heels clacking from her rushing back to her car in a near panic.

What is going on? Diego pondered, watching Esmerelda speed off.

CHAPTER 8

FREDDY PROWLED AROUND THE apartment he shared with Esmerelda. His skin itched from the animal in him trying to claw its way out. The special tea Esmeralda created to calm the creature was only pissing it off and sending him to the bathroom to piss it out. Something was riling him up, but Freddy didn't know what.

Realizing he had subconsciously stripped down to bikini briefs, Freddy had had enough. "Stop it!" He ordered.

<No. Hunt,> came the growly response in his head.

Freddy caught himself slipping off his briefs. He didn't need Esmerelda coming back from the auction to find him naked, again. "Hunt what?"

<The one that makes you betray your heart,> came the answering snarl.

Freddy's briefs fell down around his ankles. "I don't like him. I just jerked off to him a few times."

<You wish it was him,> accused the voice inside him.

Fighting the transformation, Freddy gritted his teeth. "I wish every man was him." Freddy reared back his head and howled. "Lobo! Stop it!"

<You have given up. I haven't,> Lobo snarled in his head. <I grow tired of this mortal realm. I want to go home! We heard him sing!> Lobo asserted himself over Freddy. <I'm going to get rid of the distraction. Then we'll break this curse!>

Losing the fight for control, Freddy cried out, "Lobo! No!"

The magic that eased his transformation surrounded Freddy. His body began changing. Bones and muscles rearranged and stretched under his malleable skin. Hair sprouted everywhere. His nails grew long and sharp. His mouth and nose elongated. He felt himself fading into the background.

In the span of a few seconds, Freddy was gone and Lobo had emerged, angry and snarling. Joints popped and muscles stretched as he craned his neck and arched his back. He opened and closed his paw-like hands, the deep obsidian of his nails shining in the light.

Sniffing the air, Lobo pricked his ears. "I smell him."

<Lobo, don't,> Freddy pleaded. <I haven't given up.>

"This curse must end," Lobo barked back.

Ignoring Freddy's commands to stay put, Lobo slipped out of the apartment. Lobo headed up the back stairs to the roof. Sniffing the air, he moved across the rooftop until he caught Alex's scent again. Lobo's hackles raised. He bared his teeth. He wanted to taste Alex's blood on his tongue.

Leaping from rooftop to rooftop, Lobo followed the scent as it wafted in the night air. Blending in with the night, he landed on the roof of a restaurant. He could smell the fading scent of his prey lingering about. Lobo let out a frustrated growl. The wind had scattered Alex's scent, but he had also picked up two familiar scents.

He scanned the city, following one of the familiar scents. "I know where he's going."

<Lobo, you had better not hurt them,> Freddy warned.

Lobo ignored Freddy as he made his way across the rooftops, heading toward Alex's building. The calming light of the moon did nothing to soothe the anger broiling in Lobo. The need to be free of the mortal prison was too powerful to ignore. He had had enough of the agony of the repeated death just to be born again to do it all over.

Lobo longed to go home to his pack. He wanted to return to his duty of defending the tranquil lands of Lunaray and protecting its magical creatures from the demons that sought to enslave them. It was while performing his duties that he and his pack were captured by the foul demon, Don Marcos, and then was trapped in this mortal vessel.

Freedom was so close. Freddy needed to focus on the true task at hand, breaking the curse. To do that, Lobo had to get rid of the distraction, Alex. Alex, who was now down below with the funny Diego. It would take just one swipe, and the distraction would be gone. Then Freddy would focus on what was important. Breaking the curse.

Lobo dropped down between the buildings. There he waited, crouching down in the shadows, waiting for his prey. Lobo could smell them, smell him, getting closer. Their voices were coming closer. Inside, he could feel Freddy trying to push his way to the surface to stop him.

Lobo let out a growl when the two came into view. Diego moved Alex behind him, making it easier for Lobo to pounce. Lobo heard the fear in Alex's voice when he saw Lobo's eyes staring at him through the darkness. Diego placed himself between Lobo and Alex.

Lobo stood. He stepped forward. He could not hear what they were saying over Freddy's screams in his head. Lobo moved into the light. He snarled and snapped at them, hoping to make them run and separate them. He didn't want to hurt Diego, but he would if he had to.

He snapped at Alex when he spoke. Diego moved between them. Lobo couldn't help himself. He sniffed Diego, then growled. Diego's sweet scent was tainted with Alex's foul smell. He snapped at Alex when he moved from behind Diego. The coward then used Diego as a shield as he moved away.

Lobo snapped when his prey slipped into the car, pulling Diego back into it. He lunged at the two, only to be thrown back at the feel of Diego's feet slamming into his snout. Shaking off the blow, Lobo righted himself and hurled himself back at them. He slammed into the car. The window filled with cracks from his impact.

Lobo raised his claw to slice along the car. His nails dragged across the black substance Diego wore instead of the car. Enraged, Lobo reared back and slammed into the car over and over again. He dragged a nail across the blackness. He cut through for a brief moment, only to have the blackness seal itself up again.

He slammed himself into the car over and over again, shoving the car out into the middle of the street. Huffing, Lobo slashed rapidly at the protected car. The blackness resisted him, but he could feel it getting weaker. It was only a matter of time before it would give. Then he'd have Alex.

<Stop! Do you hear that!> Freddy cried out.

Lobo stopped. His ears twitched. It was faint, but he could hear it in the distance. The voice calling to him, to them. Lobo snarled at the car, then turned his head toward the singing. He let out a howl. He had no choice. He would have to deal with Alex another time. He had to find that voice. They had to find that voice.

Lobo leaped up onto the top of the building. "He's calling to us."

<Can you tell where it is coming from?> Freddy asked hopefully.

Lobo's ears twitched about. "No. It echoes in the city." Lobo closed his eyes in concentration. "It's coming from the river area."

<What are you waiting for? Let's go!> Freddy ordered.

"Watch yourself, human," Lobo snapped.

Lobo ran across the rooftops. They could make out some of the words of the song. <Will you reach for me, reaching out for you?>

Freddy knew the song. He remembered it from a show Esmerelda watched. Fearful they'd lose this chance, Freddy urged Lobo. <Hurry! The song is almost over!>

Lobo pushed himself to his limits, barely landing on a building before projecting onto the next. "We're almost there!" They landed on a riverfront building. The hope Freddy held onto disappeared as the song ended.

"Maybe he'll sing another song," Lobo said, clinging to hope. He scanned the crowds below. He felt Freddy withdrawing inward. "If I hadn't gone after Alex."

Feeling the guilt for the part he played, Freddy admitted, <If I hadn't been pining over Alex, you wouldn't have. Come on, let's go home.>

"Esmerelda is going to be pissed," Lobo said, standing and stretching.

Cringing inwardly, Freddy said hopefully, <Maybe she won't find out.>

Finishing the song, Salvador closed his eyes. He was transported to a stage where an imaginary crowd cheered him. In that crowd was one young man, louder than all the rest, a handsome man with a sly grin and mischievous eyes looking back at him. Salvador reached out to pull him on stage with his hand. He reached out to Salvador and right as their fingertips were about to touch, the man was gone.

Since he was little and sang his first note, he was there when Salvador closed his eyes. Then, he was a child like Salvador. They had grown up together, never talking, never touching. Salvador continued singing, calling out really, for the person that completed him. It didn't matter that he probably didn't exist. The song Salvador sang was for him, for them.

Salvador left his fantasy audience and the nameless handsome man. He returned to his reality of standing on the small stage auditioning for a bar manager that wasn't paying attention. At least this woman let him sing, unlike the other bars that just turned him away. He didn't wait for a response before he started gathering his things.

He gave the woman busily tapping on a tablet a cursory glance before heading off the stage. It was these experiences that made Salvador question his choice of moving to Morgan City. He wasn't sure why he'd moved there, other than that Madame Zelda had told him that he needed to.

"Where are you going?" The dark-skinned woman asked. Tossing her short white hair to the side, she turned her attention to Salvador. "Don't you want to hear what I have to say?"

Salvador stopped mid-stride. Not hiding his bitterness, he tossed out the recycled comments he'd received since he started. "I've got a great voice and a pretty face, but I'm not the right sound or look for you. You'll keep my contact information in case you can use me in the future, but we know that won't happen. Then you'll thank me for coming in before I leave, and you'll forget about me."

"Wow," the woman said, slipping her curvy body out of the booth. "If you have mind reading or fortune telling listed on your resume as one of your special skills, I'd cross them off."

A glimmer of hope seeped into Salvador's voice. "Really? I just assumed because you never looked up from your tablet."

"You came in an hour before we opened. What did you expect?" Her hips bounced as she moved to stand in front of Salvador. "Running an upscale dive bar that the social elite likes to frequent because they like to slum it is hard work."

Salvador instantly felt guilty for having taken up her precious time. "I'm sorry. I should go and let you do your job."

She stopped Salvador with a raised hand. "You're going to hurt yourself jumping to conclusions. Yes, you have a great voice and a pretty face. No, you don't have the sound for a Friday or Saturday here, but I'm willing to give you a chance on a Thursday."

"Really?" Salvador brightened.

Her warm smile brought hope to Salvador's heart. "I've got your contact information. I'll give you a call, and I'll get you booked in a month or so."

"Oh." The elation left Salvador. "I was hoping for sooner. I just moved here."

"You need a paycheck; I need an extra set of hands that can float around the bar," she offered, feeling sorry for Salvador. "You'll sling drinks, restock the bar, work the door, and whatever else is needed. If you're interested."

Salvador's excitement bounced back up. "Yes! When can I start?"

"Tonight. You can stow your stuff in my office while you work." She offered her hand. "I'm Demona Angel. Welcome to the Hell that is the In Between."

Back in his private hotel suite, Finn stared at the orb in its small ornamental box. He wasn't sure why he was drawn to the seemingly worthless trinket, only that he had to have it. Its soft siren song had called to him in his mind, growing maddeningly louder and insistent.

Finn reached out to snatch the cursed orb, only to draw his hand back at the last moment when a strangely familiar voice shouted in his mind, <No, you fool! Use the potion!>

Finn knew that voice. It was the one that had whispered softly to him all his life, telling him what to do. The voice was raspy and as cold as ice. It was the voice that slowly crept into his own until the only difference was Finn's youthful arrogance. Now he felt that voice coiling around him.

<Use the potion I had you make,> the voice ordered firmly. <Pour it over the orb. or it will enslave you for yet another lifetime.>

Finn pulled himself away to fish out the tiny vial out of his toiletry bag. The slimy, silvery liquid swirled unnaturally in the glass, trying to get out. Curling his fingers around the tiny glass, he returned to stand before the orb that now glowed a sickly yellow.

Finn could feel the voice in his head muffling the bewitching song of the orb. Holding his hand out, Finn fought the urge to drop the vial and snatch the orb. With his thumb, he popped open the tiny cork, then turned the glass over, spilling the silvery ooze over the amber orb.

The orb pulsed angrily. The silvery sludge wrapped itself around the orb. The enticing song faded. The muck bubbled and pulsed around the orb. A loud screech came from the orb, then suddenly stopped. The silver worked its way off the orb, turning itself into a silver chain attached to the spider web cage it left around the orb.

<Yes! Free after all these lifetimes!> the voice cheered. <Quickly! Take the orb and its power will be yours!>

Finn's eyes grew wide with greed. "Power."

He grabbed the orb. Gray mist flowed out of it. The mist swirled around Finn's arm as it traveled up around to the rest of his body. He tried to drop it, but his hand would not obey. He tried to scream for help, only to have the mist fill his mouth and burrow its way down.

The voice in Finn's head cackled with delight. <Now it's time for you to awaken. Remember what you have been and know what you are now!>

Finn fell to all fours. He felt the surge of power and forbidden knowledge filling him. Memories of past lives living as a rat, scavenging for food as he searched tirelessly for Don Marcos's prison and protected it from that bitch Gitana and her mutt cousin.

Finn rose. His eyes glowed red. With a sinister smile, he raised his hand to feel the magic tingling at his fingertips. *Poor Don Marcos, cast back into Hell without his powers by his demon apprentice. Now to have a little fun.*

CHAPTER 9

"**W**E'LL BE FINE. DIEGO AND Alex just need a good night's sleep." Juan Carlos gave Aaron a gentle kiss on the lips. "Besides, I don't think you want to be here when I have my little talk with Diego."

Aaron pulled Juan Carlos against his body. "Aww, plausible deniability. I get it." He gave Juan Carlos a slow, lingering kiss. "Rain check?"

"Rain check." Juan Carlos groaned, reluctantly pulling away. "Ugh, are you sure you want to date a single mother?"

Aaron laughed. "Yes. Don't be too hard on Diego. He meant well. Just tell him he's never allowed to call me 'daddy,' okay?"

"That title is reserved for me." Juan Carlos said with a smile. He gave Aaron another kiss, then patted him on the chest. "Go. Before we give these boys a sex education lesson that will scar them for life." Aaron gave Juan Carlos a salacious grin. Laughing, Juan Carlos playfully ordered, "Go!"

"Call me tomorrow." Aaron winked and walked away.

Juan Carlos appreciated the view of Aaron walking away before closing the door. His happy smile turned to a look of seriousness when Juan Carlos turned to face the two men sitting cozily on the couch. It would have been a touching sight if they didn't have important things to discuss.

"Now that my night has been ruined and I've sent my date home," Juan Carlos said, taking a seat, "is there anything you two would like to discuss?"

Alex looked at Diego, then at Juan Carlos. "Um, how about that werewolf thing that attacked us?"

"To be fair, it was more interested in you than it was me," Diego clarified. "Are you sure you didn't do something to piss it off?"

Insulted, Alex accused back, "Well, it really seemed to like you."

"I'll have Esmerelda look into it. I don't think we'll be seeing it again," Juan Carlos dismissed their banter.

Diego turned his attention to Juan Carlos. "Okay, let's talk about Esmerelda and Freddy. Why were they my backup at the gym? Why did

Esmerelda show up looking for Freddy? Where was Freddy?"

"The creature was obviously supernatural, so I called an expert. She must have called Freddy, and since Freddy and the creature were gone when we got there..." Juan Carlos waved his hand in a circle, encouraging them to draw their own conclusions.

Diego recognized the gesture for what it was, a ploy to avoid telling the truth. Knowing he would get nowhere with Juan Carlos, he turned his attention to Alex. "How long have you known I am Shadow Guardian?"

"I, uh, um, started suspecting after I made the modifications to your suit," Alex admitted. "I wasn't sure if it was you or Juan Carlos at first. Then I realized Juan Carlos didn't have the body."

"Excuse me?" Juan Carlos asked, offended. Alex gestured to his body, then to Diego's. "Okay, I'll give you that one."

Alex continued, "Then Diego kissed me, and that's when I sort of knew. That's why I went to the gym to see if Shadow Guardian would show up." Alex paused. "That creature was there that night."

"You must be mistaken. Esmerelda didn't say anything about a creature, just that they found you passed out."

"No. It was there. I remember those eyes. It was there." Alex's brows knitted together in concentration. "It's foggy, but I remember. I ran into the alley in case Diego, err, Shadow Guardian, needed help."

Diego patted Alex's leg. "Aww, that's so sweet. Don't ever do that again."

"I have a feeling I probably will." Alex patted Diego's hand. "Anyways, I have a vague memory of it growling at me, then running, and then, then I woke up in my bedroom."

"Esmerelda and Freddy found you passed out and took you back to your apartment. They didn't say they saw anything else in that alley." Juan Carlos quickly added before side-tracking the conversation. "Anyways, now that Alex knows that you're Shadow Guardian, you don't have to worry about how you are going to tell him."

"I wasn't going to tell him," Diego blurted out.

Alex turned and stared at Diego. "You weren't going to tell me?"

"No, of course not. It's called a secret identity for a reason," Diego explained arrogantly.

Alex huffed, "You don't trust me."

"Of course I trust you. This is just different," Diego tried to explain.

Alex scowled at Diego. "Different? Different than telling me about how Freddy made you feel like part of the family on his birthday when he shoved the cake in your face?"

"Wait. What?" Juan Carlos jumped in. "Freddy never shoved cake in Diego's face. What is he talking about, Diego?"

Crossing his arms, Alex turned to face Diego. "Yes, Diego. What am I talking about? Why is throwing Freddy a birthday party so important?"

"Um, well," Diego stumbled. "Okay, it didn't quite happen the way I told you."

Juan Carlos shook his head. "Because Freddy threw Diego an over-the-hill party for his thirtieth birthday and he wants revenge."

"I want to throw him a funeral birthday." Diego grinned. "I already ordered the coffin."

Alex narrowed his eyes at Diego. "Really? You couldn't tell me the truth? Again?"

"I'm going to bed." Juan Carlos stood up. "I guess I won't be needing my earplugs tonight."

Through clenched teeth, Alex responded, "Yes, you will. I'm going to be yelling at Diego for a while."

"Don't forget to yell at him for asking Aaron if he was going to be his daddy," Juan Carlos reminded Alex. "Then tell him he'll be meeting with Mr. Andrews and his son alone on Monday."

Diego nearly jumped from the couch at the news. "What? You know I can't stand them! Where will you be?"

"I'm leaving tomorrow to take care of personal business out of town. I'll be back Monday evening." Juan Carlos flashed an impish smile at Diego. "I can't wait to hear how it goes."

Juan Carlos went to his room, leaving Diego to get yelled at by Alex. He was relieved that he was able to steer the conversation away from Freddy. He hated keeping secrets from Diego, but it was for the best. These were matters that were beyond them, and Esmerelda couldn't have Diego interfering as he would inevitably do.

Juan Carlos stopped at the door to his room and listened to the two fighting. He sighed. He knew what he had to do. "Alex, if you forgive him, you'll be able to make up!" Juan Carlos called out, then added, "In bed!" Juan Carlos closed the door to his bedroom before he had to hear the sounds of them making up.

CHAPTER 10

DRAPED IN THE HOTEL ROBE, FINN relaxed on the hotel couch, taking in the view of the two slumbering naked young men in his bed. They were easily lured here from the app with the promise of Finn's twinkish body and sexual release. Little did they know the price they would pay was their mortal essence.

Don Marcos was a fool for feasting on purity when the carnal pleasures are so much tastier, Finn mused, running a hand down his smooth chest. *It's been so long since I've had a human body, I had almost forgotten how much fun they can be, and hunting is so much easier now that you can order in.*

Finn's thoughts were interrupted by the groaning of one of the young men stirring to life.

With a flick of his wrist, he sent the man back into slumber. *I'm not ready to deal with you yet.*

Feeling the grumblings of his empty stomach, Finn decided to take full advantage of his new body. It had been way too long since he'd enjoyed food that he didn't have to scavenge. Now that his consciousness was awake in this human body, he was going to enjoy all the worldly pleasures Don Marcos had denied him by trapping him in that rat body.

Finn retrieved his phone from the robe pocket. After logging into the hotel's app, he ordered himself something to eat. As an afterthought, he ordered something for his two new tasty morsels. They would need their strength for when he needed them again, but first, he would need to enthrall them.

Finn's hand found Don Marcos's former prison dangling around his neck. The magical power trapped inside was slowly trickling into him. It would take time for him to absorb all the power from the prison that had been turned into a mystical charm. He had to be careful because he was vulnerable until then.

Finn left the comfort of the sofa to stand beside the bed. He could smell the alluring scent of hedonism wafting off the two young men. He was tempted to gorge himself on their succulent essence, but foolish gluttony would only complicate things. He had spent too many lifetimes preparing for his return to screw it up now.

Lifetime after lifetime, he had spent in the body of a rodent protecting Don Marcos's prison. Each lifetime, he slowly siphoned away a tiny bit of Don Marcos's power. It was the power that Don Marcos had used to lure him into a false apprenticeship. Power Don Marcos had used to bind Finn into that wretched form to prevent Finn from becoming his rival.

Finn stretched his arm out over the two men with his fingers splayed. With power in his voice, he softly said, "Mine." Tiny red ribbons drifted down from Finn's fingers and took root in the unconscious men. "Mine," Finn repeated, pushing his will into them, imprinting the desire to serve and please him. He felt them yield to him. They were his now.

Finn withdrew his hand from above the two men. The exertion of the simple spell had left him far too weak for his liking. The desire to pull from his new chattel was interrupted by the knocking on the door. Cinching up his robe, he crossed the suite and opened the door to yet another delectable morsel.

"Room service," the slender young man announced. "Where would you like it, sir?"

Finn gave the chipper man a once over. He couldn't have been much older than the body Finn now occupied. The white pressed shirt and black slacks he wore, along with his shellacked black hair parted to one side, gave him an air of professionalism and innocence that Finn knew to be a lie.

With a lecherous smile, Finn stepped aside. "Come in, come in."

Finn could taste the indulgence that flavored this man as he passed by. Closing the door, Finn followed the young man into the suite. He watched the man glance over at the bed as he lifted the domes off the serving dishes. Finn casually placed a hand on the bellhop's shoulder.

Sending a pulse of desire into the bellhop, Finn asked, "What are you doing later?"

"Hopefully, you," he answered quickly. Finn felt a similar pulse of desire pulse back into him. "That is, if you want someone who won't tire so easily."

Finn's lips curled slightly into a smile. This bellhop had potential that he could exploit. "What's your name?"

"Dante." He turned and slipped an arm around Finn's waist. Pulling Finn close, he said, "My shift ends at noon. I do offer other services when I'm off the clock."

Finn felt a surge of power flow into him from Dante. *He has the potential and doesn't even know it.* Finn gently pushed away from Dante. "Come back after your shift, and we'll see what services you can perform for me."

"Will those two be involved? Because that's extra." Dante motioned with his head to the two men passed out in the bed.

Finn slipped away from Dante and the temptation he presented. The boy didn't know what he was. Few do until their potential is unlocked. Finn returned to the sofa, laying, so his robe opened just enough to tempt. "You don't need to worry about them. You're only coming back here for me."

"Just so you know, how you left those two is how I normally leave men." Dante came around the cart and handed Finn the electronic bill.

Finn took the bill and signed it with a generous tip. "I can't wait to see what you can really do."

"I can't wait to show you." Dante took the bill back without looking at it. "I'll see you at noon."

Finn was about to continue the banter when his phone rang. He mentally cursed when he saw who was calling. "The sperm donor." Finn groaned. "We'll continue this when you return." Dante gave an over-exaggerated bow and left. Rolling his eyes, Finn answered the phone. "Hello, Father."

"You'll have to entertain yourself for the day," his father barked into the phone gruffly. "I'm not feeling well, and I need to prepare for our meeting tomorrow at DJC."

Finn knew what that meant. He was hungover and probably had an escort or two he picked up that hadn't left yet, and needed to sleep it off. At any rate, it saved Finn from having to deal with his father today. "That's fine. I can entertain myself today."

"Make sure you're ready for the meeting tomorrow. You need to pay attention. You're next in line to take over the company when I step down." Finn rolled his eyes at the comment. "And if that rude woman comes around again wanting to buy that silly bobble you had to have, make sure you sell it to her at a hefty price."

Finn jumped from the couch. He clutched the orb dangling from his neck in fear when the memory of the woman came back to him. "Oh, she'll pay a hefty price if she comes around again."

"Good. I'm going back to bed. Stay out of trouble," Finn's father said before ending the phone call.

"The Gitana," Finn snarled. He moved toward the bed. With a wave of his arm, he ordered, "Awaken."

The two men on the bed stirred to life. Getting out of the bed, they looked around glassy-eyed until they found Finn. Finn raised both hands and said, "Mine." The tiny red ribbons zipped through the air into the two men. He reinforced their desire to serve him.

Feeling their obedience firmed up, Finn ended the spell and lowered his hands. "Clean yourselves up and get something to eat. You have work to do finding me a place to reside in this pathetic city."

CHAPTER 11

A LEX LAY ON THE COUCH STARING at the screen of his tablet, trying to decide what changes the code needed. Aside from the occasional tap of Alex's finger, the apartment was cozily quiet. Diego was downstairs in his private gym working out, and Juan Carlos had yet to emerge from his room.

Alex wasn't sure why Juan Carlos had deemed this a high priority or why he gave strict orders not to make a simulation. The complicated code was from one of Dr. Gingerman's projects that was deemed too dangerous to continue. All Juan Carlos would tell him was that it was for hypnosis.

Alex set aside the tablet and closed his eyes. He was too tired to make sense of the code. He'd work on it later. Maybe he'd get Diego to help him. Diego did owe him for the fight last night and the debacle that was dinner. Diego had protected him from the wolf creature, but he had thanked Diego more than enough for that privately last night.

Alex was right at the cusp of drifting off for his mid-morning nap when a large, sweaty, hard body landed on him. Alex cracked his eyes open to see Diego's grinning face. He wanted to be annoyed with Diego, but he couldn't help himself. He smiled back at the playful man on top of him.

"Eeww, you're sweaty." Alex playfully tried to push Diego off him.

Diego waggled his eyebrows. "You didn't mind me being hot and sweaty last night when—"

"Diego!" Alex cut him off quickly. "Get off me! I'm still mad at you."

Diego stuck out his lower lip, pretending to pout. "But you forgave me last night."

"That," Alex said with extra emphasis, "was so we could have make-up sex. Now I'm mad at you again."

Pretending to be offended, Diego gasped. "You used me for sex? How could you?"

"Oh, don't even." Alex laughed. "Now get off me, you stink. Go take a shower."

Getting off Alex, Diego asked, "Come join me?"

"No," Alex said firmly, crossing his arms. "I'm still mad at you."

Diego stuck out his lower lip. "If you forgive me, we can have make-up sex."

"Is that all you want? Sex?" Alex asked in a huff.

Diego looked off into the distance and began rubbing his chin. "No." Diego snapped his fingers in realization. "Chocolate chip cookies!" Diego made his eyes go wide with excitement. "Are there chocolate chip cookies?"

"No." Alex started laughing when Diego slumped his shoulders in disappointment. "Okay, okay. I'll forgive you, now go take a shower. Juan Carlos should be up soon."

Diego cocked his head in confusion. "He left this morning while you were still sleeping."

"What?" Alex asked, sitting up. "I wanted to ask him about this code before he left."

Diego's tone turned serious. "You shouldn't be working off the clock. This is your free time, not company time. You should be spending it with me at home. You can work on that tomorrow when you're spending time with me at work."

"Okay." Alex popped up off the couch and pecked Diego on the lips. "What time are you taking me back to my place?"

Diego put an arm around Alex's waist. "About that." Alex tensed. "I think you should stay here until we figure out what the wolf thing wants with you."

"Okay." Alex relaxed. He was safer in the luxury penthouse. "But I still need to go get some things."

"I can buy..." Diego paused when he saw the scowl on Alex's face, "...us something great for dinner tonight."

Alex patted Diego's chest. "Good boy. Now get your stinky butt in the shower." Alex pulled himself away from Diego. "I'll make you some fresh coffee."

Diego sniffed under one arm and then the other. "You're right. I do stink."

Alex headed to the kitchen to make coffee while Diego went to his room to shower. Alex laughed when he saw Diego stop and wiggle his butt. It still amazed him that he and Diego were an item or that he was bold enough to kiss Diego in the office that day. They made such an odd, yet perfect, pair.

Alex laid back down on the sofa, determined to get a little rest in while he waited. After Diego found out Alex knew about him being Shadow Guardian, he took Alex into the Shadow Guardian command center as an apology. Alex saw where the Shadow Guardian suit repaired and recharged itself. He also got to see all the secret projects he was working on for Shadow Guardian and where Juan Carlos monitored Shadow Guardian when he was out on patrol.

Alex was like a kid in a candy store looking at the various gadgets and gizmos. It was nearly two in the morning when they finally went to bed. They both went into full tech mode, with Diego showing off his ideas and creations while Alex fawned over them. They would have spent all night in the secret command center had Alex not started yawning.

"Wake up, sleepyhead." Alex yawned and stretched at the sound of Diego's voice. He fluttered his eyes open to see Diego coming from the kitchen with two steaming cups of coffee. "I made it just the way you like it. Hot, sweet, and caramel brown. Like me."

Sitting up, Alex yawned and stretched. "I'm guessing I'm not going to get a real nap in today, after all."

"Well," Diego said, carefully handing Alex his coffee before sitting down. "I was thinking that since Juan Carlos is out of town and you know that I'm Shadow Guardian, I thought maybe you could man the command center while I patrol."

Alex couldn't contain the excitement in his voice. "Really? That would be awesome. Do I get a special suit or code name?"

"No special suit, but you can get a code name." Smirking, Diego set his coffee down. "How about the mean boyfriend who won't forgive me?"

Alex shot Diego a playful, annoyed look. "How about the sweet boyfriend who has every right to be mad and will be taking it out on his boyfriend all day?"

"How about Shadow Voice?" Diego quickly asked. "That sounds sexy and powerful."

Alex mulled it over his head. "Yeah, I like it. What will I be doing?"

"Monitoring my suit and vitals. Checking the screens for any alerts." Diego put an arm around Alex. "Maybe it can be our thing. That way, Juan Carlos can spend more time with Aaron."

Alex leaned against Diego. "That sounds like a great idea, but I definitely need to get a nap in."

"We'll go get your things from your place, then come back here for a power nap," Diego suggested.

Alex snuggled against Diego. "Okay, you're forgiven. One hundred percent."

"No takebacks?" Diego prodded playfully. "No takebacks."

Alex yawned. "Until I want more make-up sex."

CHAPTER 12

ESMERELDA LOOKED DOWN AT Freddie, softly snoring in his bed. She had zoomed across the city looking for him, only to find him back in the apartment sleeping. Under normal circumstances, she would have woken him up, but these weren't normal circumstances. She knew how taxing the mystical transformations could be.

That was last night. This was the morning after, and the relief Esmerelda had felt at finding him sleeping was gone. Esmerelda had an entire night to let her concerned worry transform into loving anger. Now it was time for Freddy to wake up and face that loving anger.

Esmerelda twirled her wrist and raised her hand. Freddy lifted up off the bed. When he was two feet off the bed, she closed her hand into a fist.

Freddy's body fell like a lump onto the bed. When Freddy didn't wake, she repeated the process. It was after the third time that Freddy woke up.

"Coño, Esmeralda. You know I need my sleep after transforming," Freddy grumbled, wiping the sleep from his eyes. Seeing the disapproving glare from Esmeralda, he added, "Can I at least put shorts on before you read me the riot act?"

Esmerelda chewed her bottom a moment before saying, "You have one minute. Don't forget to wake up your partner in crime, too. I have words for you both." Esmerelda turned and left. When Freddy entered the living room, Esmeralda stopped pacing. She pointed at the sofa and ordered, "Sit!"

"Can I at least get some juice or something before you yell at me?" Freddy asked, plopping down onto the couch.

<Tell her it was your idea,> Lobo whimpered. <There's no need for her to be mad at both of us.>

Freddy shook his head. "I'm not telling her that!"

"Oh, good. He's awake." Esmeralda pulled a blue and purple powder from her pocket. Raising it in the palm of her hand to her mouth, she blew it onto Freddy. It swirled around Freddy and then coalesced into a sparkling outline of Lobo beside him. "I have words for both of you."

Lobo looked at his arms and grumbled, "Why does she always have to make me sparkle?"

"At least you're not the one who," Freddy sneezed, "has to have powder blown in their face."

Lobo snarled, "I look like some glittery wolf go-go boy."

"Hey, don't hate on go-go boys. Dancing at bars paid the bills for a few years." Freddy defended.

Lobo shot back, "You just liked dancing in your underwear on the bar."

"That I did," Freddy responded with a big grin. "Maybe I should see if any of the bars are hiring. It was fun."

"Are you two done?" Esmerelda interrupted. They turned their attention back to Esmerelda. "You two have some explaining to do. Why did you transform? Why did you go after Diego? Where did you go after? Oh, and you both need to thank Juan Carlos for covering for you."

Lobo answered timidly, "We didn't attack Diego. We were after Alex."

"You were after Alex," Freddy corrected. "You forced the transformation."

Lobo snarled back, "I wouldn't have forced the transformation if you hadn't given up on breaking the curse."

"I didn't give up," Freddy argued. "I was just being real. My thirtieth birthday is in a few weeks, and we haven't broken the curse."

Lobo snapped, "You were lusting after that Alex man."

"I wasn't lusting after Alex!" Freddy exclaimed. "Okay, I was, but I was only using him as source material!"

Esmerelda closed her eyes and shook her head. "I really wish we weren't so open with each other." Taking a deep breath, she moved on. "That doesn't explain why you transformed or where you went."

"Lobo decided to remove Alex from the picture." Freddy gave his shiny partner a dirty look. "He forced the transformation."

Lobo grumbled under his breath, "Tattletale."

"Lobo, you know you're not supposed to transform without me!" Esmerelda scolded. Hearing Lobo whimper, she added, "Don't play the innocent pup card. We all know you haven't been innocent or a pup in five thousand years."

"Tell her about the singing." Lobo prodded Freddy in hopes of diluting Esmerelda's anger. "Tell her we heard him."

Esmerelda's voice went soft with sympathy. "You hear him every lifetime, but the curse keeps you two apart. Don't you understand? Breaking this curse is the only way—"

"He's here. In the city." Freddy cut her off. "We tracked his singing to the waterfront."

Seeing the determination in both of their eyes, Esmerelda decided to lay all her cards on the table. "I found Don Marcos's prison, and I need your help getting it." Esmerelda pretended not to be worried at how similarly they both perked up. "I didn't see Don Marcos's rat minion anywhere, but I felt him."

"Why didn't you get it?" Freddy asked, on the edge of his seat.

Esmerelda sneered. "Some rich twink outbid me, and he wouldn't sell it to me."

"No," Freddy said immediately.

Lobo began chuckling.

Esmerelda sighed. "Freddy, he has Don Marcos. I need you to—"

"No," Freddy repeated.

Lobo continued chuckling.

Determined, Esmerelda continued, "Freddy, just seduce the twink and steal the orb."

"No," Freddy said more vehemently.

Lobo started laughing harder. "Tell her why."

"Shut up." Freddy tried to punch Lobo, but his hand went through the mystical illusion.

Esmerelda looked at Lobo, then at Freddy. "Tell me."

"Tell her, or I will," Lobo threatened merrily.

Esmerelda stared at Freddy until he finally broke. "Fine. The last time I was with a twink, he kept calling me 'daddy.'"

"Tell her what happened when you told him to stop calling you 'daddy.'" Lobo was laughing uncontrollably now.

Freddy gave Lobo a dirty look. "He started calling me 'papi.'"

"That's," Esmerelda covered her mouth to hide her smile, "horrible."

Freddy glared at her. "It's not funny."

"It's a little funny." Esmerelda was doing her best to contain her laughter.

Freddy growled. "Laugh it up."

Esmerelda grew serious. "Well, suck it up. I don't care if he calls you 'daddy,' 'zaddy,' 'papi,' or 'papi chulo,' I need you to seduce him and steal that orb so I can finally cast Don Marcos into Hell."

Freddy slumped back into the couch. "Fine. I'll do it." Freddy looked over at Lobo. "But he has to promise not to go after Alex again or anyone else I, um, use as source material."

"Lobo," Esmerelda said sternly, crossing her arms and staring pointedly at Lobo's sparkling form.

Lobo snarled, "Fine."

"And no more transforming without me there," Esmerelda added.

Lobo huffed, "Fine."

"With that settled, how about helping me get my apartment ready today?" Freddy asked. "We've been putting it off way too long."

Esmerelda gave him a worried smile. "You know you can manage the apartment from here." Freddy gave her an incredulous look. "Fine. Get some breakfast, and we'll head over."

"That was amazing," Finn said, laying back in the bed and playing with the orb around his neck. He had absorbed a great deal of the power from it, thanks to Dante.

Dante slipped his underwear on and stood. "Yeah, that was fantastic. Too bad I have to go." He pulled on his pants. "Will that be cash or electronic payment?"

"Neither. I think it's time you quit your menial job and side hustle," Finn said blissfully. "You should stay here with me. Be my," Finn thought for a moment, "personal assistant."

Dante laughed while slipping on his shirt. "What, are you going to make an honest man out of me?"

"No," Finn answered. "I want you just as you are, by my side, ready to assist me in whatever I need."

Dante chuckled as he buttoned up his shirt. "What sort of needs would those be?"

"What do you know of the mystical arts?" Finn asked, getting out of bed and slipping into his sleep pants.

Dante sat down on the bed to put on his shoes. "Do you mean like card tricks or street magic?"

"More like turning someone into a rat, summoning demons, or turning people, like the two idiots you saw in my bed earlier, into devoted servants." Finn made red sparks dance on his fingertips.

Dante jumped back in shock. "How did you do that?"

"I told you." Finn wiggled his fingers. Tiny red ribbons of energy flowed through the air to dance around Dante. "Magic. Real magic."

Dante recoiled until he felt the feather-like touches on his exposed skin. "That's really cool. What else can you do?"

"Stick around and find out." Finn stopped the ribbons at the sound of his phone notification going off. Taking his phone off the nightstand, he smiled when he saw the picture he had been sent. "Looks like my new minions have found us the perfect love nest. Shall we go check it out? That is, if you're accepting the position."

Dante smiled impishly. "How can I turn it down?"

"Good." Finn winked at Dante. "On our way to our debaucherous love nest, you can quit your job here and inform your other clients that your services are no longer being offered."

With a hint of deviousness in his voice, Dante asked, "Can you teach me any of that?"

CHAPTER 13

SHADOW GUARDIAN LEAPED FROM building to building toward Alex's apartment. It was too early in the night to do a proper patrol, so he was strictly doing reconnaissance. The creature that had attacked them the night before had been lying in wait for Alex, and there was a good chance the stupid beast would be doing the same tonight.

"Shadow Guardian to Shadow Voice," he said into the coms. "How's it going? Are you getting used to the controls?"

Alex tried to keep his tone professional, but the excitement leaked into his voice. "Shadow Voice here, so far, so good. I think I've got everything, but I'd like another lesson just to be sure. Hey, what does this button do?"

"Don't!" Shadow Guardian screamed as he tucked and rolled onto a rooftop. "Never ask what a button does and then press it without waiting for an answer."

Alex guiltily responded, "Okay."

Landing on the top of Alex's building, Shadow Guardian went into a crouch. "We'll have Juan Carlos teach you when he gets back."

Alex buzzed in his ear again. "Where did he go?"

"I'm scanning the rooftop now." Shadow Guardian tapped his temple to activate the visual sensors. "Look for anything unusual," he ordered before saying, "I don't know. He didn't say, and after that dinner, I wasn't going to make him mad by asking."

Alex shouted into Shadow Guardian's ear, "Wait! The ledge by the alley—are those claw marks?"

"I think so." Shadow Guardian moved to the ledge. Examining the strange cuts to the building, Diego voiced his thoughts. "These are claw marks, but they aren't canine. It looks like it has opposable thumbs. Do you remember anything about its claws?"

He heard the shudder in Alex's voice when he answered, "Only that they were long and sharp. No, that was his teeth. I don't think I got a good look at its claws. What do you remember?"

"I remember it had big ears," Shadow Guardian recounted.

Alex chimed in, "The better to hear you with."

"It had big eyes," Shadow Guardian continued.

Amused, Alex said, "The better to see you."

"And then those big teeth," Shadow Guardian went on.

With a slight chuckle, Alex said, "The better to eat you with, my dear."

"Did you," Shadow Guardian paused. "Did you just quote Little Red Riding Hood?'"

Shadow Guardian could hear Alex holding back his laughter. "You did set me up."

"Focus." Shadow Guardian was grateful Alex couldn't see him roll his eyes. "I'm going to check out the alley." Shadow Guardian climbed over the ledge. Activating his grips, he moved down the building. "He must have jumped down from the roof. I'm not seeing any damage to the side of the building."

Worry permeated Alex's voice. "Are we sure this is a good idea? I'm not an expert on the controls yet. Maybe we should wait for Juan Carlos."

"I would, but I think he's hiding something about this creature." Shadow Guardian answered as he moved quickly down the building wall. "He's been deflecting my questions, and he started that argument with us last night."

Alex was silent on the line for a moment before he responded, "He did, didn't he? I wonder why he did that."

"Because he's hiding something." Shadow Guardian dropped the last few feet to the ground. "I don't see any damage to the ground, either. Let's hope we can find stray hair or something that will give us a clue about what that thing was."

Alex's voice grew serious. "Okay, start looking around."

Shadow Guardian moved around, turning his head from side to side to let the optical scanners do their work. *There's been too much time since the attack.* Shadow Guardian debated about what he was going to do next. He had discussed it with Alex. It was dangerous, but they needed answers.

"Keep your eyes open," Shadow Guardian ordered. His suit began flooding the air with Alex's scent. "If he's around here, this will draw him out."

"What did you do?!" Alex asked in a panic.

Finding a dark spot in the alley to hide, Shadow Guardian calmly answered, "I just flooded the alley with your scent."

"What?!" Alex screamed over the radio. "Why? We said we'd wait to do that!"

Scanning the alley for movement, he said, "We need answers, and there's only one way to get them."

CHAPTER 14

FREDDY LOOKED AROUND THE apartment. He was almost settled. It had been a blank canvas when they had arrived that afternoon, but now it was becoming another one of his masterpieces. With the random pieces of furniture donated from family and his art decorating the apartment, the place felt like it was his.

Esmeralda left after she placed her protection spells and made Freddy promise to leave before Alex came home. With everything aligning to break the curse, neither of them had faith that Lobo could keep his word about not attacking Alex if he caught his scent. Lobo didn't understand the difference between lust and love, since his kind mated for life.

Deciding to truly make this place his own, Freddy pulled his shirt off and tossed it aside. He turned to a blank page in his giant sketch pad and locked it into place on the easel. Closing his eyes, he let inspiration guide him. What he needed to create started to take shape. The lines and colors coalesced in his mind.

Without opening his eyes, he reached over to his charcoals and paints. Freddy let the feeling take him. When he opened his eyes, they were glazed over. He snatched one of his charcoals, then drew a black line across the white paper. A moment later, his hand was flying over the paper.

The sun had been setting when he started. Three hours later, he had gone through the entire sketch pad. His body wore the smudges of exertion. Gathering his sketches, he went to the couch to look them over. Every single sketch was of Freddy's mystery man living his daily life. He didn't know if they were past, present, or future images.

There was one of him singing in a bar for a solitary woman. Another of him walking down the street at night. The next was of him sleeping alone on a mattress on the floor. They went on through his day. It was the last one that gave Freddy pause and stirred Lobo. He was talking to Esmerelda.

Freddy studied the picture. *Where is this? When is this?*

<It has to be now! Or soon!> Lobo shouted in his head. <We need to go! Now!>

"I can call her." Freddy picked up his phone from the table. "Besides, I'm not meeting the man of my dreams covered in charcoal."

<Hurry!> Lobo paused. <Wait. What is that smell?>

"Control yourself, Lobo. You promised." Freddy winced at the press of Lobo pushing his way to the surface.

<He's scenting his territory,> Lobo growled. <He's scenting you!>

"People don't do that!" Freddy argued in vain. He pressed call on Esmerelda's contact on his phone right before he dropped it to the floor.

Lobo's rage bubbled to the surface. <That pathetic beta needs to be put in his place!>

Freddy stood. He let out a soundless scream of pain as Lobo slashed his way to the surface. His bones popped and snapped. His muscles tore themselves apart and stitched themselves back together. His skin ripped as the fur began sprouting all over his body.

Lobo stood in the shredded remains of Freddy's clothes. His body trembled with the urge to attack. He threw his head back and let out a cry of challenge, drowning out the frantic cries of Esmerelda screaming on the phone as it shook the building.

Lobo sniffed the air. He had Alex's potent scent. Leaving the apartment, he followed the smell of Alex out of the building. He ignored the shrieks of terror from people on the street. Alex's smell led into the alley he had hidden in last night. Alex's scent was strong, almost overpowering.

Lobo peered into the darkness of the alley. He saw no one, but he smelled Alex. He cautiously walked into the alley. He sensed something was amiss. The alley smelled as if it were bathed in Alex's scent. He cautiously moved further in. His eyes darted about, trying to find Alex.

Lobo was halfway down the alley when his ears picked up the muffled sound of a heartbeat. He stopped when he caught movement in the shadows. A figure rose out of the darkness. Gray swirls flowed over the body. Lobo's nostrils flared. He looked like Shadow Guardian, but it smelled like Alex.

<Lobo! Stop! That's Diego!> Freddy cried out fruitlessly.

Lobo snarled menacingly.

"Okay, puppy. It's time to put a muzzle on you." Shadow Guardian took a fighting stance.

Alex's smell grew stronger. It was coming from Shadow Guardian. Lobo growled. He bared his teeth and flexed his claws. His hackles raised. Rage filled Lobo at the impudence of a basic male marking the alley with his scent in an attempt to lure Freddy away.

"Let's see how you like being on a leash." Shadow Guardian thrust out his arms.

Two black tendrils shot out from Shadow Guardian's arms at him. Lobo jumped high into the air, narrowly avoiding the attack. Landing in a crouch, he charged Shadow Guardian. Shadow Guardian attempted to evade him by doing an acrobatic flip. Lobo reached up and caught him by the arm, and hurled him against the building.

"You won't escape me, Alex." Lobo snarled. "I'm going to teach you not to go sniffing around someone else's mate."

Picking himself up off the ground, Shadow Guardian said, with a wince, "So the big bad wolf can speak." Getting into a fighting stance, he added, "I'm not Alex, but I'm going to make sure you keep your paws off him."

"Where's Alex!" Fangs bared and claws drawn, Lobo attacked.

This time, Shadow Guardian stood his ground, grabbing Lobo's wrist and twisting until it was pinned behind his back. Before he could break free, Shadow Guardian pressed a hand to Lobo's back. First, there was a tingle from the touch, then a pop of shock as electricity jolted through him. Then, he felt the crash of the wall into him.

The electrical attack stopped, and Shadow Guardian released him. Lobo turned to face Shadow Guardian. Rage filled him, drowning out Freddy's pleas to stop. Shadow Guardian stood poised to strike again. Lobo flexed his claws.

Lobo was about to strike when Shadow Guardian spoke. "Give up, big bad wolf. You'll find this little piggy is made out of brick."

<Okay, you can give him one good smack for that line,> Freddy chimed in, finally able to break through Lobo's confusion.

Perplexed, Lobo asked them both, "What does that even mean?"

"Don't worry about it." Shadow Guardian thrust his left arm forward to send out one of his black tentacles. Lobo jumped to avoid it, but Shadow Guardian had predicted that movement. From his right arm came another, catching Lobo's foot. Shadow Guardian yanked. Lobo was pulled, smashing down into the ground.

Lobo looked up to see Shadow Guardian standing smugly ten feet away. He had withdrawn the tentacle from his left arm, but the one from his right was still tightly wrapped around Lobo's ankle. Lobo rose up on all fours. Lobo bared his teeth in a grin. He would teach Shadow Guardian a lesson for being cocky.

Lobo pushed himself off of the ground. Flipping in the air, the tendril to Shadow Guardian pulled taunt. Shadow Guardian was lifted in the air. The tentacle released. Lobo landed in a crouch. He watched Shadow Guardian tuck into a ball, then unfurl to land in a similar position, blocking the entrance to the alley.

Lobo was about to charge again, but he paused when he saw Esmerelda standing in the alley entrance. She twirled her hands. A thick mist started filling the alley. Shadow Guardian stood. Before he could turn to see her, Esmerelda lifted her right hand to send a tiny blue orb of magic out, striking Shadow Guardian in the back.

Momentarily stunned, Shadow Guardian fell into the mist. Briefly, Lobo thought to pounce on the incapacitated Shadow Guardian, but he caught Esmerelda's furious glare before the mist engulfed them both. Knowing there would be Hell to pay later, he leaped up onto the roof and made his way back to Esmerelda's.

Esmerelda sat on her couch, scrolling through the search results on her tablet. She was trying to distract herself from Freddy being at his new apartment alone, so close to where Alex lived. It wasn't that she didn't trust him. It was Lobo that she worried about. He was becoming a loose cannon. That's why she cast the alerting spell along with the protection ones.

She had spent the last few hours researching the rude young man and his father. She needed to find them so Freddy could seduce the twink. Then he could steal the orb, and they'd end the curse. They were so close, but the only thing of importance she could find was they didn't live in Morgan City.

She set the tablet aside and immediately began worrying about Freddy. She knew he needed this time alone. Between taking over the management of DJC properties and planning for this fundraiser, they were on top of each other at home. That and she was checking up on him every free moment.

The real worry was Lobo. She didn't trust him. Not since the night they were providing backup for Shadow Guardian when he took down the three bears. Lobo would have attacked Alex had she not stepped in. She was certain of that, especially after the incident last night. She had to get him back under control.

Esmerelda felt a tingle. One of her spells was activating. The one she had cast to alert her if

Freddy transformed. Jumping up from the couch, she grabbed her phone just as a call from Freddy came through. For a moment, she was relieved, thinking the spell had malfunctioned. She had never hated being right so much.

"Freddy?" she said into the phone. When no response came, the panic began to rise in her. "Freddy?! Freddy, talk to me!" The familiar sounds of Lobo emerging came through the phone. "Lobo! You promised!" She screamed frantically, grabbing her keys and rushing out the door. The string of threats and curses she let out was lost in Lobo's thunderous howl.

She felt her tracking spell activate when she got behind the wheel of her car. *Thank the stars. He's only a few blocks away.* She drove with a cautious sense of urgency through the nearly deserted streets.

She slipped into a parking spot a few buildings down with the precision of a professional stunt driver. Esmerelda was a good ten feet from her car before the beep of her car alarm intruded on the clack of her heels as she rushed down the street.

She followed her tracking spell toward the apartment building. *Thank the stars, he hasn't gone far.* Her relief was short-lived. She saw Lobo and Shadow Guardian facing off. She ducked behind the wall before they noticed her.

She heard Shadow Guardian say, "Give up, big bad wolf. You'll find this little piggy is made out of brick."

What does that even mean? She thought as Lobo spoke her thoughts aloud. She peered around the corner to watch Lobo lift himself up off the ground and sling Shadow Guardian up in the air as he flipped. Shadow Guardian tucked into a ball and landed in a crouch with his back to her.

Shadow Guardian stood. Lobo looked ready to charge. *I have to act now.* She moved into the alleyway. She swirled her hands at her side, gathering energy. Softly she said, "Neblia."

A foggy mist began filling the narrow space. She pulled a small amount of energy into her right hand. A tiny blue orb formed. She lifted her arm up and sent it flying. It hit Shadow Guardian in the back, momentarily stunning him and sending him falling into the misty clouds.

Lobo caught her angry glare. She gathered more energy, prepared to strike Lobo if he tried anything foolish. *Try it, furball.* Magic crackled on her fingertips. The fog engulfed them. From her tracking spell, she sensed Lobo leaping up into the air, then heading back toward her apartment. *I'll deal with him when I get home.*

Esmerelda stored the energy she had gathered to end the fog spell. She waited until she saw

Shadow Guardian's dark form standing in the mist before she casually walked away. She had enough to deal with without having to explain everything to Shadow Guardian.

Moving down the street, she continued to magically track Lobo. He was almost back to her apartment. They'd be sleeping by the time she got back. Freddy was always drained after a transformation, and Lobo would be cowering away from her. She was pondering ways to keep Lobo under control when she collided with a young man leaving the building in front of her car.

"I'm so sorry, I..." Esmerelda trailed off as she got a good look at the young man. She didn't know him, but she felt that she did. "Do we know each other?"

The blonde man pushed his bangs from his eyes. "It's okay, totally my fault." He looked at her quizzically, as if he sensed the same thing. "No, I don't think so." He offered his hand. "I'm Salvador. Salvador Libertad."

"Esmeralda. Esmerelda Cesar Romero." She said, taking his hand.

A vision came with the touch. It was a flash, brief and blurry, but she saw Salvador singing. He was on a stage with people cheering. He reached out into the crowd to pull someone up on stage with him. Right as she was about to see who it was, it ended.

"You're a singer," she said before quickly adding, "I have a gift for spotting talent."

If Salvador was thrown off by her statement, he didn't let on. "I am. Well, a struggling singer."

"I have a feeling that will change." Esmerelda pulled a card from the fold of her dress. "Here. I'm doing a fundraiser. I could use some fresh talent."

"Thanks." Salvador looked at the card with awe before saying with a slight hint of urgency, "I'm sorry, I have to get to work. It was a pleasure meeting you." Salvador rushed down the street. He yelled back, "I'll call you!"

It's okay if you don't. She slipped back into her car. *That card is enchanted. You'll never lose it, and I'll be able to find it wherever you go with it.* Esmerelda smiled. Starting her car, she pulled out into the streets. *I better call Juan Carlos and let him know what happened.*

CHAPTER 15

"**I** CAN'T BELIEVE THOSE INCOMPE-
tent thralls thought that hovel was appro-
priate for me," Finn grumbled while lounging on
the couch of the penthouse apartment.

Dante handed Finn a Cosmo. "That's why you
have me." He joined Finn on the couch, careful
not to spill his own. "Those peons had no sense
of taste. I'm glad you sent them away. The place
they found wasn't on the top floor, and it didn't
have a bar. Idiots!"

"Yes." Finn sipped his tart drink. He eyed
Dante suspiciously. "Tell me, how did you find
such a perfect place filled with young, virile men
that fornicate more than rabbits?"

Dante proudly answered, "My 'daddy' owns it."

"Your father owns this building? Then
why were you working at the hotel?" Finn felt

something amiss in the pit of his stomach. The laugh Dante let out didn't ease that feeling. He gathered his power, ready to strike down Dante. "What's so funny?"

Dante's lips curled into a coy smile. "Not my father. My 'daddy.'" Dante downed the last of his drink. "He's an older gay man that helps me out from time to time and gives me money."

"And what do you give him?" Finn asked bitterly.

Dante put a comforting hand on Finn's leg. "Just my company. Nothing more. I swear."

"Okay." Finn relaxed a bit. He tested his connections to the men in the building. Finn felt their carnal acts flooding him with energy. "Did I enthrall everyone? Could we have missed anyone?"

Dante's tone turned to one of admiration. "Every single one of them. Your power is amazing!"

"That it is." Finn stored the power he gathered. "I need to return to the hotel before my father comes looking for me. We have that stupid meeting tomorrow."

Dante sulked. "Okay, but will I get to see you after?"

"Of course," Finn answered sweetly. He needed to bond Dante to him, and quickly. Earlier, he had felt the twinges of the Gitana and her wolfman using their magic. It wouldn't be long before they felt the power he had stolen from Don Marcos growing and came looking for him.

"I have an idea." Finn set the remains of his drink down. "Why don't we get married?"

Dante's eyes filled with delight. "Are you serious?!"

"Deadly. I know what I want, and I want you." Finn wrapped an arm around the naive man. "Let's do it as soon as possible. We can do something big later."

Dante squealed with delight. "I can't believe this! We need to get rings! Oh, there's so much to do!"

"Is that a yes?" Finn asked.

"Yes! Yes! I'll marry you!" Dante jumped up from the couch, pulling Finn with him. "I'll take care of everything! Come on! We need to go out and celebrate!"

"Where are we going?" Finn asked, a hint of amusement in his voice.

Pulling him into the bedroom, Dante said, "You'll see!"

Salvador arrived at the In Between with only a few minutes to spare before his shift started. Herc, the muscular black man with dreads that worked the front door, nodded at him as he passed. Behind the bar was Ryuu, a squat, muscular Asian man with smooth caramel-brown skin and silvery eyes.

Tonight, Salvador's job was to get Ryuu whatever he needed: beer, ice, glasses, or more alcohol. They weren't expecting a big crowd since it was Sunday night. The music was already playing, some Indie Rock, that was just loud enough to be heard but low enough to allow for casual conversation.

"Salvador, a word," Demona called to him right after he clocked in behind the bar.

Salvador ducked back under the bar and meekly headed toward Demona. "I know I was cutting it close, but I'm not late."

"No, you're not," Demona responded coolly. "We have special rules here." She paused unexpectedly. She studied Salvador for a moment. "Did you meet anyone recently?"

Salvador thought nothing of the question as he began babbling excitedly. "Yeah! I ran, literally, into this woman outside my building. She said she had a gift for spotting talent and asked me to perform at her fundraiser." Salvador pulled Esmerelda's card from his pocket. "She gave me her card. I was going to tell you about it later to see what you thought."

"May I see the card?" Salvador willingly handed the card over. "Esmerelda Cesar Romero." Demona said the name like it left a bitter aftertaste in her mouth. Salvador thought he saw sparks when Demona ran her thumb over the card. "She's a good person. Passionate and hotheaded sometimes, but she's a good person. Call her when you're ready." Demona handed back the card. "You'll be ready Wednesday."

"Wednesday?" Salvador questioned, taking the card back.

A playful smile formed on Demona's stoic face. "Yes, and be sure to give her my regards. It seems like a lifetime since I've seen her. Go on, get to work."

Baffled, Salvador headed back to the bar to help Ryuu. He spent the next two hours with the quiet, smoldering man learning how to set the bar up correctly, keep it stocked, and run the register if need be. The one thing Salvador couldn't master was moving around the bar without colliding with Ryuu. It amazed Salvador how the hulking man seemed to slip around him with barely a touch.

People started trickling in as soon as the doors opened. Salvador did his best to keep from being underfoot as Ryuu greeted each patron by name and made their orders with a flourish. Bottles were tossed in the air and spun as he poured the drinks. Not a drop was spilled or a bottle dropped.

By midnight, there were thirty or so people in the bar. Things were just slowing down when two young men came up to the bar. Ryuu stiffened when he saw them. He didn't address them by name and made their drinks without any fanfare. He didn't relax until he saw Demona standing at the booth they sat in.

"To our engagement." Dante raised his glass.

Finn raised his glass in turn and forced a smile. "To our engagement."

After sipping their cocktails, Dante reached out and played with the bobble that hung around Finn's neck. "This is an odd piece of jewelry, but it suits you."

"I've been trying to get my hands on it for such a long time." Finn put his hand over Dante's. He felt the sudden pulse of power surge into him.

Dante leaned in to kiss Finn, but they were interrupted by a curvy black woman with silky white hair. "Gentlemen, since this appears to be consensual, I'll allow it this time. The next time you enter my bar, obey the rules, or I'll enforce the oath you signed in order to enter. Understood?"

"Understood," Finn sneered. "Now, may we enjoy the celebration of our engagement?"

The woman did an over-exaggerated bow. "By all means." Then left the table.

"How dare she threaten me?" Finn seethed. "Once I'm at full power, I'm going to come back here and teach that mutt some manners."

Dante turned Finn's head to face him. "Don't let her ruin our evening." He gave Finn a wet kiss on the lips. "I hate that we can't spend the night together. Are you sure I can't just come up to your hotel room?"

"There's nothing I would like more, but that cretin that calls himself my father would throw a fit." Finn returned the kiss. "He's going to be enough of a headache when he finds out I won't be leaving with him."

Dante giggled sinisterly. "Wait until he finds out we're getting married."

"About that, I want it fast-tracked. Do whatever you have to." Finn cut his eyes at Demona. "I want us married as soon as possible."

Dante winked. "I'll have my 'daddy' pull some strings. He has connections high up."

CHAPTER 16

DIEGO ARRIVED AT WORK STILL feeling the dull ache from his encounter with the creature he and Alex had dubbed Big Bad Wolf. With the encounter last night, there was no doubt in either of their minds the beast was after Alex. Now they had the revelation that someone was working with or controlling the creature. Someone created that fog and shot Shadow Guardian in the back.

"I can't believe you did that to Juan Carlos and Aaron. On second thought, I can. You did blackmail me." Rolling her eyes, Dion handed him a message. "That's from Juan Carlos about today's meeting."

Diego flashed a mischievous smile. "How are you and the barista?"

"I'll be getting my coffee somewhere else now." Dion sighed. "She brought a date to our date. The only way it could have been worse would have been if you were there asking her if she was going to be your new mommy."

Diego hung his head in embarrassment. "I'm not going to live that down, am I?"

"Diego, you asked Juan Carlos's date if he was going to be your daddy." Dion started laughing. "You've got to admit that's hilarious."

Diego started laughing. "If that didn't scare Aaron away, nothing will."

"Speaking of scary encounters, remember you have the meeting with that chauvinist Daniel Andrews and his demon son." Dion shuddered. "The last time they were here, he told me to be a good little girl and get him some coffee. Then that little brat of his sneezed into his hand right before he shook Juan Carlos's hand."

"Make sure there's lots of hand sanitizer in the meeting room." Diego grimaced.

"Three bottles." Dion crossed her arms.

Diego thought for a moment. "I think this might be a good test for the liquid medical gloves I came up with."

"I'll have one of the prototypes sent to Alex's office." Dion began furiously typing away at her computer. "I'll let you know when he has it set up for you."

Diego tapped Dion's desk. "Thank you. Remind me to give you a raise." Diego headed into his office.

"The paperwork is in your inbox," Dion called back to Diego.

Sitting at his desk, Diego read the note.

> Today is just a formality to sign the papers for the deal we have already agreed to. If Daniel Andrews tries to change anything now, walk away from the table. I have backup suppliers.
>
> Make sure you come home right after work. I have a surprise for the family.
>
> Love,
> Juan Carlos

Diego put the note into the paper shredder by his desk. He pulled up the files for today's meeting. He didn't just dislike Daniel Andrews; he hated the man. The pompous jerk was always trying to price gouge them or slip some sneaky clause in. If it wasn't for the fact that they were the biggest supplier of chemicals in the country, Diego would have insisted they cut all ties with them.

Maybe I can get them to cut ties with us. A mischievous smile spread across Diego's face. He pressed the button to call Dion. "Dion, how would you like a temporary promotion and an extra week's vacation?"

Standing outside the conference room, Dion flexed her fingers. "This stuff better come off."

Diego put a hand on her shoulder. "It will. I'm almost certain of it."

"Diego! What do you mean you're 'almost certain?'" Dion asked, panicked. "We stripped down to our underwear and you had Alex spray us down!"

Diego chuckled. "There's a special solution that he'll spray on us after that'll dissolve it, then we'll simply shower, and it'll be gone."

"It better." Dion took a deep breath and straightened her shoulders. "Come on, let's do this."

Diego gave her a wink before opening the door and stepping through. "Gentlemen, thank you so much for waiting." Diego forced his brightest smile at the two men. He saw the irritation on the older man's face as he struggled to stand. "Mr. Andrews." Diego offered his hand.

"Where's Juan Carlos?" Daniel Andrews asked, ignoring Diego's outstretched hand. "And who is she?"

Dion thrust her hand out beside Diego's. "Dion Holiday, acting chief of operations while Juan Carlos is out on personal business."

"Pleasure to meet you." Finn took Dion's hand when the terse moment looked as if it was about to explode.

Diego saw a moment of shock, then confusion on Finn's face. He held onto Dion's hand longer than normal, then used his other hand to give her a two-handed shake. Diego saw the hint of a sneer before Finn finally let go and repeated the process with him.

When it was obvious that Daniel Andrews wasn't going to take either of their hands, Diego took his seat and asked, "Shall we get started?"

"When will Juan Carlos be back?" Daniel Andrews asked curtly, as he sat down. "I will only work with him."

Dion answered coolly, "He did not specify a return date."

"Then we'll pick this up when he returns. I expect to be compensated for this waste of time in the agreement I do sign." Daniel Andrews snapped.

Diego tapped the screen of the tablet in front of him. Deepening his voice, he spoke in an authoritative tone. "I am the CEO of this company. You'll either sign this with me, or you can walk away from the table."

"I will remind you that this agreement has to be signed today in order for you to be the exclusive supplier for our chemical needs." Dion tapped away on her tablet. "The exclusivity agreement you signed with us expires at midnight tonight."

Diego was taken aback when Finn spoke, his voice peppered with anger and annoyance. "Just sign the agreement so we can get out of here, Old Man."

"Remember your place, boy. You're not the owner of my company yet!" Daniel Andrews turned his anger toward Diego and Dion. "I will not sign an agreement with a glorified secretary or her man-child boss. Tell Juan Carlos this insult will cost your company dearly. Just try and find a supplier able to meet your needs."

Diego grinned smugly. "Juan Carlos already has a list of suppliers ready to put in bids."

"Just sign the agreement, you fool!" Finn ordered. "If you don't, the company will be out millions!"

Daniel Andrews stood abruptly. "You can tell Juan Carlos to double the price when he comes begging me to sign a new deal. Come on, Finn. I'll deal with you in the car."

Daniel Andrews stormed out of the conference room. Finn sat a moment, seething, before wordlessly following. Shocked, Dion and Diego turned to look at each other. A satisfied grin spread across both of their faces.

"Well, that was quick and painless." Dion stood and gathered the tablets. "Let's wash this stuff off and get to the real work." When she noticed Diego still sitting and watching her, she asked, "What?"

"You've been with the company almost since the beginning. I think it's time you moved on from, as Mr. Andrews put it, a glorified secretary." Diego paused. "I need you to find and train your replacement." Dion's eyes went wide with uncertainty. Diego stood. "I'm going to talk with Juan Carlos about your actual new title, but," Diego extended his hand, "congratulations on your promotion."

CHAPTER 17

"**W**AIT UNTIL JUAN CARLOS hears about how those two treated me!" Daniel ranted in the back of the car. "He'll have their heads!"

Finn ignored him. He was busy going through the business reports of their company. *Idiot! What has this man been doing? I chose this body to be reborn into, so I could live in luxury! The company is on the verge of collapse!* Finn set his phone down. Glaring at his father, he shouted, "Will you shut up!"

Daniel paused mid-tirade. He stared at his son. The surprise at Finn speaking to him in that manner quickly morphed into anger. "How dare you talk to me like that! Isn't it bad enough you embarrassed me back at DJC? You had better get your attitude in check by the time we get back to the hotel!"

"I said, shut up!" Finn's eyes flared red. *If only we weren't genetically related, then I could enthrall him.* He waved his hand, causing Daniel's lips to clamp shut. "Now listen, you foolish old man, your little temper tantrum back there cost our company millions. Millions that it desperately needs to stay afloat. A dead monkey could make better business decisions."

Finn grew tired of watching his father paw at his mouth, trying to open his lips. He waved his hand again and said, "Sleep." Daniel's eyes closed, and he slumped in his seat. He was grateful the privacy screen was up so the driver couldn't see what all had transpired. Finn dialed Dante's number.

"Hey, babe, how's it going?" Dante's chipper voice both irritated and delighted Finn.

Feeling a need to vent, Finn began, "The twit I call my father blew the deal. All he had to do was sign. Instead, he made a spectacle of himself, then left!"

"Oh, no." Finn heard genuine concern in Dante's voice. "What are you going to do?"

Finn looked over at his "father." He couldn't leave the man sleeping forever. It would take a constant stream of magic to maintain the curse. It was bad enough that Finn was feeling the irritation of the curse he inherited when he started absorbing Don Marcos's power. It was a steady, irritating, weak stream from the curse cast on two men an eternity ago.

"I'm not sure," Finn admitted. "He cannot be left to run the company, and I can't control him."

There was a pause before Dante asked, "Don't you inherit the company if he dies?"

"Yes," Finn answered with a huff. "But who knows when that will be."

Finn loved the deviousness in Dante's voice as he said, "Sometimes an accident can be an unhappy son's best friend."

"Accident." Finn liked the way the word rolled off his tongue. Letting the subject fall to the wayside, he asked, "How are the wedding plans going?"

There was a slight tinge of disappointment in Dante's voice. "The bad news is that the earliest we can get married is Wednesday, but the good news is that Mayor Trainer is going to perform our ceremony."

"I'm going to dump this man that considers himself my father off at the hotel. Then I'm checking out of the hotel and coming to the apartment." Finn looked out the window, trying to trace the faint string of magic that trickled out. "I have an itch that needs to be eliminated."

"I'll have something special to feed your hunger when you get back. See you soon." Dante clicked off.

Finn lay in the king-size bed of the penthouse apartment with Dante's head on his chest. Dante was playing with the now useless bobble that hung around Finn's neck that once imprisoned Don Marcos. All the power was drained, but he still wore it because Dante liked to play with it.

Finn feasted on the surge of carnal pleasure from the ten or so men fornicating in the main room. He could feel that their zeal was slowly ebbing. He fought the temptation to gorge himself and leave them as lifeless husks. The one thing he did learn from Don Marcos was the importance of maintaining his chattel.

With a casual flick of his hand, Finn freed the men and allowed them their release. He moaned in delight at the burst of carnal energy. Finn ran his hand down Dante's back. He reached out to his enthralled slaves. Through his connections, he selected four for his needs.

"Did you decide what you wanted to do about your father?" Dante asked, playing with the orb.

Finn closed his eyes and stretched out with his mind. He felt the tug of the curse he had cast on his father. "I extended his stay to Thursday. I have brown-nosing idiots at home running damage control." Finn kissed the top of Dante's head. "I haven't decided what type of accident my father should have yet. There can be no question about the cause."

"I'm sure you'll think of something," Dante purred. "I'm going ring shopping tomorrow. Did you want to come?"

Finn felt the annoying trickle from Don Marco's curse resurface. He needed to end the curse. He needed all his power for when, not if, the Gitana and her mystical mongrel dog came for him. "No, I have very important errands to run. Just make sure it's the highest quality gold."

"That's going to cost money." Dante pouted. "Money I don't have."

Finn patted Dante's back. "I had you added to my accounts and named my heir." Finn was no fool. Dante was his insurance policy. If anything happened to this body, he would be able to take over Dante's body once they were bonded. "Don't go crazy. Until we're married, I want us to keep a low profile."

"Anything you say," Dante said, snuggling close to Finn.

CHAPTER 18

SALVADOR SAT ALONE AT HIS SCAVenged kitchen table with mismatched chairs. He had a few more hours before he had to go to work. A song was forming in his mind, but he couldn't find the words or the music for it. He could hear it in his mind, waiting to be created, to be captured on the recording app on his phone so he could share it with the world.

"Ugh!" Salvador cried out. He locked his phone and set it aside. He turned his attention to the wilting plant on the table. "I can't come up with a new song, and I can't keep a simple plant alive." He ran his fingers over the limp leaves. He tried humming a few bars of the melody in his head.

Salvador stood and went to the window to look out over the city. What he wouldn't give to be like the people down below. They knew who they were and where they came from. They had families and histories. Salvador didn't have any of those. What he had was a story, a promise, and a quirky woman who raised him.

The woman who raised him, Madame Zelda, told him that he magically appeared in a basket on her doorstep. She named him Salvador because that was the name stitched in golden thread on the blanket with him. She said the very moment that she laid eyes on him, she knew it was her destiny to protect and nurture him. That since she was the queen of the Gitanos, he couldn't wish for better.

Salvador would sit for hours listening to her spinning tales of his previous lives. He knew every story by heart. There was magic in her words. In his heart, he knew they had to be true, though he pretended not to believe them. He couldn't explain it, but he drew strength and courage from those stories.

Salvador closed his eyes and he was transported back. Madame Zelda was sitting in her beat-up and broken lounger with her black hair streaked with gray flowing around her. She had a warm smile on her aged-lined face. A steaming hot cup of tea that she would sip during the story was sitting on the small table beside her. She pointed at the spot on the rug with her knotted wood cane for him to sit. She was going to remind him of his destiny.

"Salvador, you are an old soul. Not as old as mine, but not many are as old as mine," Madame Zelda said with a wink. "Your story started out many, many years ago, when the demon Don Marcos decided to feed upon your torment by separating you from your true love." She picked up her tea. She blew the steam away before taking a sip. "Before he could, you met the love of your life."

She winked again. "We'll just say you knew him intimately, and that ruined you for him. You were bonded with that man, and Don Marcos's evil power couldn't break it." She paused to take another sip. "Enraged, he wanted to banish your soul across the ocean. To your true love, he tried to imprison one of the mythical creatures so he could force it to do his bidding."

Madame Zelda's smile grew wide when she said the next part. "The Gitana foiled his plans. Sort of." Another sip of her tea. "They were young and not yet trained. With their partner Felix by their side, they were able to trap the foul demon and free the longing souls from their prison." Her voice went somber after that. "They weren't strong enough to stop the curse before it took hold."

She looked Salvador pointedly in his eyes. "With the love in both your hearts and two kind souls, the Gitana was able to change it. They put in a loophole, as you young people like to say. In doing so, they unknowingly infused you with power." She winked at him. "Do you remember what she said?"

"Sing for him." Salvador heard himself saying.

Madame Zelda smiled proudly. "That's right. Sing for him. Lifetime after lifetime, you have sung for him. Each song brought the two of you closer and closer. That little seed of magic grew in your soul, and now it is waiting to burst free and bloom."

Then she did something that she had never done before. She leaned forward. "Salvador, feel the magic in your voice." She tapped him on the forehead. It was in his mind, but Salvador felt it. "Bloom." Then this strange tingling feeling spread from the touch. "Find the Gitana, Salvador. Find her, and you find your true love."

Salvador opened his eyes. He opened his mouth and sang his scales. He felt something new as the notes left his mouth. Finishing his scales, he returned to the kitchen table. He was about to pick up his phone when he noticed his plant. The leaves were a full and vibrant green. He watched the tiny red blooms open.

Salvador ran a finger over a leaf. "What the Hell?"

CHAPTER 19

RIDING UP IN THE ELEVATOR TO the penthouse apartment, Esmerelda tried to come up with some reasonable explanation to give Juan Carlos about Lobo attacking Shadow Guardian last night. The truth was, she didn't have one. The only person who might be able to was Freddy, and he was in no condition to give anyone answers.

After the transformation last night, he was completely drained. He couldn't even make it to his bed. She had found him passed out on the floor. She had gotten him into his bed, then headed to bed. She would deal with Freddy and Lobo once they woke. When she checked on them a half hour ago, they were still sleeping.

Steeling her nerves, she stepped out of the elevator into the penthouse apartment. The group text Juan Carlos had sent asked everyone to be there at five. She was there early to explain everything the best she could before the others showed up and to be able to leave if Juan Carlos asked her to. She didn't want to ruin the surprise Juan Carlos had for everyone with her's and Freddy's problems.

Stepping into the foyer, she heard the sounds of two men chatting. One voice belonged to Juan Carlos, the other she recognized but couldn't place. She moved further into the apartment, stopping in the entryway to the living room. Juan Carlos was on the couch. Across from him, with his back to her, sat the other man.

Juan Carlos's eyes brightened when he noticed her standing there. Standing up, he merrily said, "Esmerelda, you're early."

The other man rose and turned. Esmerelda felt the breath leave her body. She knew that face. It was older. Hardened by life, but his eyes still held their soft gentleness. She couldn't believe it was him standing there in a crisp white polo and Khaki pants, with the same vibrant tattoos decorating his arms.

"Hello, Esmerelda." She felt her body tremble when he spoke. "It's good to see you again."

Esmerelda covered her mouth. Her eyes welled up with tears. When she said his name, it was almost a whisper. "Gato." She wasn't even aware her legs had given out until she felt strong arms lifting her up from behind.

"Are you okay?" Esmerelda looked up into the worried face of Aaron Heath. "Let me help you to the couch."

Esmerelda steadied herself. "I'm fine, thank you. I was just not expecting..." She looked over at Gato.

"Me." Gato finished for her.

She let Aaron guide her to Juan Carlos and Gato with a hand on her lower back. "Thank you, Aaron." She turned to look at the man that had spent the last ten years in prison for protecting her. Her lip trembled when she said his name. "Gato."

"Let's leave them to catch up." Juan Carlos motioned for Aaron to join him in the garden.

Once they were alone, Gato said, "You look good." Esmerelda could hear the nervousness in his voice. "I've missed you."

"I- I-" Esmerelda flung herself at Gato. Hugging him, she cried into his chest. "I'm so sorry I never went to see you."

Gato put his arms around her. "I didn't want you to see me in there." Holding her tight, he said, "I did get all of your letters. That's what got me through."

"Oh, Gato." Esmerelda looked up at him with tear-filled eyes. "If only I hadn't been a fool back then."

Gato wiped away a tear from her cheek. "If only I had been the man you deserved back then."

"You were." Esmerelda leaned in for a kiss. Gato did the same.

"Gato!" Esmeralda and Gato pulled away at the sound of Diego's voice. "When did you get out?"

Fidgeting, Gato answered, "This morning."

"Diego, we should find Juan Carlos," Alex said, tugging at Diego's arm.

"He's outside with Aaron." Esmerelda nodded to the garden.

Letting Alex pull him outside, Diego called back, "We'll catch up later!"

Shaking his head, Gato said in disbelief, "I can't believe that's the skinny little boy that used to goof around with Freddy."

"Wait until you see Freddy." Esmerelda laughed. "Those little boys grew up to be two very fine young men."

Gato took Esmerelda back into his arms. "You and Juan Carlos deserve the credit for that."

"Why are we talking about them when we should be making up for lost time?" Esmerelda leaned in for a kiss.

"When we get up there, I'm going to take Juan Carlos aside and tell him about the encounter last night," Diego instructed Alex in the elevator. "I'll tell him it was all my idea."

Alex cocked his head at him. "It was your idea."

"Right, that's the story we're going with." Diego nervously loosened his tie. "I need to tell him right away."

Alex took Diego's hand in his. Giving it a squeeze, he said, "Relax. I know Juan Carlos is your parental figure and all, but he's not going to flip because you went out as Shadow Guardian with me at the helm."

"I'm talking about the encounter with the Big Bad Wolf." The doors to the elevator opened. "He's not going to be happy that we went hunting for him."

Stepping into the foyer, Alex asked, "About that, what was that line about being a little piggy made of brick about?"

"It was a three little pig thing." Diego shook his head. "I'll come up with something better next time."

Alex casually bumped Diego on the shoulder. "You're not harvesting my pheromones again. Those microbots tickled."

"Is that?" Diego pulled Alex along with him into the living room. "Gato! When did you get out?"

Pulling away from Esmerelda, Gato started fidgeting. "This morning."

"Diego, we should find Juan Carlos." Alex pulled on Diego's arm.

Esmerelda nodded to the garden. "He's outside with Aaron."

"We'll catch up later!" Diego called back as Alex pulled him outside into the garden.

Once outside, Alex asked, "Who is Gato?"

"Diego! Alex!" Juan Carlos called to them from one of the shaded benches. "Over here!"

"I'll tell you later," Diego said, through a fake smile. "Keep Aaron busy for me?"

"You mean Daddy Aaron?" Alex teased as they made their way over.

Diego nudged Alex. "Go ahead, call him that to his face."

"What did you think of my little surprise?" Juan Carlos asked, beaming. He looked over and asked, "Are they playing nice?"

Diego winked at Juan Carlos. "We kind of interrupted them playing nice." Diego gave Alex's hand a squeeze. "Alex? Didn't you have something private to ask Aaron?"

"Oh, yeah. It's, um, quite personal," Alex said, flustered.

Aaron stood and stretched. "Okay, let's go pretend to talk so these two can talk."

"Sounds good. Have a nice chat, boys." Alex pecked Diego on the cheek. "Come on, Aaron. Let's be somewhere else."

Diego sat down beside Juan Carlos. "I have something to tell you," he said once he was sure Aaron and Alex were out of earshot.

"You're going to ruin my day, aren't you, niño?" Juan Carlos groaned.

Diego sucked in his lower lip before saying, "I sort of gave Alex a crash course in the Shadow Guardian room, and I went out on patrol last night."

"And?" Juan Carlos asked.

Diego took in a deep breath before blurting out, "I went back to the alley where we saw the wolf creature. He showed up and attacked me. A strange fog filled the alley, and then I got shot in the back from some sort of energy blast."

"What?!" Juan Carlos stood. He glared into the penthouse at Esmerelda. "He attacked you?! Esmerelda needs to answer some questions!"

Confused, Diego stood up. "Um, what does she have to do with this? I thought you would be mad at me."

"I am." Juan Carlos glared back into the apartment. "I need to have a little chat with Esmerelda."

Juan Carlos stormed back toward the apartment. Diego stood dumbfounded for a moment before he followed. Out of the corner of his eye, he saw Aaron and Alex doing the same. They all burst in right as Gato and Esmerelda were about to kiss. They pulled away when they saw everyone there.

With fury in his voice, Juan Carlos asked, "Esmerelda, why did Freddy attack Diego last night?"

"I didn't." Freddy appeared in the doorway. Diego noticed he seemed drained. "Lobo did."

Freddy leaned against the wall of the hallway leading to the living room. He knew he should be in bed, but after reading the group text, he knew he had to come explain. He owed apologies, if they would take them, for Lobo's actions over the past two nights. Esmeralda was about to kiss someone when Juan Carlos came bursting in, trailed by Diego, Alex, and Aaron.

"Esmerelda, why did Freddy attack Diego last night?" Juan Carlos angrily accused.

Freddy stumbled into the doorway. He felt so weak, but he found the strength to project his voice. "I didn't. Lobo did."

"Freddy!" Esmerelda cried. She moved to go to his side, but Freddy waved her off.

All eyes were on Freddy, but he zeroed in on the man with Esmerelda. "Gato. It's good to see you." Freddy tried to take a step into the room, only to stumble. Diego rushed to his side, catching him before he hit the floor. "Thanks, Diego."

Everyone was silent while Diego helped Freddy to the couch. "I'm guessing you guys want some answers." Freddy weakly smiled at everyone.

"Freddy, you don't—" Freddy held up a hand to keep Esmerelda from talking.

Aaron looked around nervously. "Should I be here for this?"

"You lost plausible deniability the moment you started dating Juan Carlos," Alex answered.

Diego let out a sound of frustration. "Would someone please tell me what's going on? How was Freddy able to lift those huge planters like they were nothing? Why did the soil have to be hand mixed, and why couldn't Freddy touch it? Why was Esmerelda looking for Freddy when that creature attacked, and why did Juan Carlos say he chased it away? Why did he just say Freddy attacked me?"

"It's complicated," Juan Carlos answered sharply. "Keep an open mind."

"There's more to it than you know. Everyone, please sit down." Freddy turned his attention to Esmerelda. "It's time to come clean. About all of it."

CHAPTER 20

EVERYONE SAT IN SILENCE AFTER Esmerelda and Freddy had finished their story. Diego sat there, processing everything. The reborn souls, the evil demon, Esmerelda actually having magic, Freddy having another being in him, and the quest to find some unknown lover so they could break the curse.

It was Juan Carlos that broke the silence. "You're telling me that Freddy doesn't transform like you told me. That he has a second soul in him that emerges, and he's the one responsible for attacking Diego and Alex?"

"Yes," Freddy answered. "His name is Lobo."

"I want to see him," Juan Carlos demanded. "I have words for him."

Diego piped in, "Wait, are we just glossing over the fact that Freddy and Esmerelda knew I was Shadow Guardian and that we just told Aaron and Gato?"

"We'll get to that later," Alex said, patting Diego on the knee. "So, behind the gym, in the alley..."

Freddy finished, "Yes, that was Lobo about to attack you."

"I then cast a sleep spell on you, stopped Lobo, and then Freddy and I took you back to your apartment," Esmeralda finished.

"Why doesn't Lobo like me?" Alex continued.

Esmerelda and Freddy looked at each other before looking back at Alex. Freddy started to answer, "It's because I used you as, um..."

"Source material," Esmerelda finished for him.

"Source material?" Alex thought about it for a moment, then his cheeks grew flush with embarrassment. "Oh! Oh! Let's never talk about that again."

Puzzled, Diego asked, "Source material?"

"I'll explain later." Alex patted Diego's leg.

Aaron started shaking his head. "I really shouldn't have been here for all this."

"Eh, at least I'm not some mystical magic thing or a rich gay man running around in some super suit." Gato shrugged.

Diego's eyes widened with excitement. "Wait! You could be my sidekick! You could be Shadow Cat! You know, because your name is Gato?"

"I'm not going to be your sidekick," Gato groaned.

Alex scowled at Diego. "Why does he get to be your sidekick?"

"I really shouldn't be here for all this," Aaron said, putting his face in his hands.

Having had enough, Juan Carlos shouted, "Enough!" The room went silent. "Diego, they would have learned eventually. Alex, no one is being anyone's sidekick. Aaron, it's not a big deal. We haven't broken any laws. Technically. Now, can we move on?"

"Yes, please." Esmerelda took Freddy's hand in hers. "Freddy needs his rest."

"We need to meet Lobo," Juan Carlos declared. "Diego, will you take Alex to the safe room?"

"No need to do that. You can meet him without him actually being here." Freddy looked over to Esmerelda. "Do the trick."

Esmerelda gave Freddy's hand a squeeze before standing up. Standing in front of Freddy, she reached into the pocket of her dress and pulled out the mystical powder. "Gentlemen, meet Lobo." She blew the glittery pink powder onto Freddy.

The powder swirled around Freddy. He sneezed twice. The powder swirled faster around Freddy. He sneezed again. The sparkling powder stopped, then pulsed before moving to swirl beside Freddy. The outline of Lobo's form shimmered into place.

Lobo looked at everyone, then at himself. "Pink? Hhmm. I like it."

"It talks," Aaron said in disbelief.

Lobo snarled at him. "I'm not an 'it.' I'm a 'him.' Remember that, or I'll bite your face off."

"Why did you attack Alex and Diego?" Juan Carlos jumped in.

Lobo looked over at Freddy. "Didn't you tell them already?"

"Yes," Freddy groaned.

Lobo scratched his sparkling head. "Then why is he asking?"

"I don't know," Freddy answered.

Lobo cocked his head at Juan Carlos. "Do I need to explain what Alex being source material means?"

"No!" Alex blurted out.

Annoyed, Diego asked, "What is source material?"

"Later!" Alex and Juan Carlos responded almost in unison.

Lobo gave Diego a toothy grin. "Diego, I didn't see you there."

"Focus!" Esmerelda demanded. "Lobo, why did you break your promise last night and go after Diego?"

Lobo raised an eyebrow in confusion. "I didn't go after Diego last night. I went after Alex. I smelled Alex."

"We did. It was like, really strong. Lobo said it was like Alex had marked his territory strong." Freddy added.

Diego and Alex looked at each other before Diego explained, "That's because I flooded the alley with Alex's scent to try and trap you."

"You did what?!" Esmerelda, Freddy, Juan Carlos, and Lobo shouted at them.

Alex recoiled. "We thought it was a good idea at the time."

"That's what drove Lobo crazy right when I was going to call Esmerelda about that man I drew her with," Freddy grumbled.

Gato nudged Aaron. "Can you believe this?"

"I really shouldn't be here for this," Aaron repeated.

Esmerelda stayed focused on Freddy. "You drew me with a man?"

"It was him." Lobo perked up his ears.

"That's why I was still in the apartment." Freddy clarified. "I started doing charcoal sketches. I went into the zone, and forty drawings later, I was done."

Esmerelda dropped to one knee and took Freddy's hand. "What were the drawings of?"

"It was like his day, and the last one was of you with him," Freddy explained. "I was about to call you when," Freddy cut his eyes to Diego, "someone provoked Lobo."

Esmerelda's eyes grew wide with excitement. "I did meet someone that night after I blasted Diego in the back."

"You shot me in the back!" Diego exclaimed.

Esmerelda glanced over at Diego. "Sorry."

"You met him?" Freddy asked, wide-eyed. "Did you get his name? Do you know where he is?"

Esmerelda gave him a weak smile. "His name is Salvador. He's a singer."

"Where is he?" Lobo asked excitedly.

Esmerelda patted Freddy's hand. "I don't know. I gave him one of my cards so I could track him, but..."

"But what?" Freddy narrowed his eyes at her.

With an apologetic tone, she said, "He went into In Between."

Lobo let out a howl of dismay.

"No!" Freddy covered his face in defeat.

Confused, Gato asked, "What is In Between?"

"It's a bar of sorts," Esmerelda answered.

Diego shrugged. "So, we go to the bar and see if they know him. Problem solved."

Lobo growled. "Someone got us banned from that bar for all eternity."

"That was my previous life," Esmerelda quickly added. "I was young, and if I remember correctly, you were the one making the bartender uncomfortable."

"What?" Lobo shrugged. "He was hot. How was I supposed to know he was an asexual dragon?"

"Because he told you," Freddy argued.

Lobo shrugged. "He also said he could swallow me down easily."

"He meant literally." Esmerelda shook her head. "He told you that you'd look good roasting with an apple in your mouth."

"This is too much," Aaron moaned. "Werewolves. Magic. Asexual dragons."

Juan Carlos offered his hand to Aaron. "Let's go get you a drink."

"Okay," Diego said once Juan Carlos and Aaron left. "I got to know. Am I the only one that wants to play fetch with Lobo or get him a squeaky toy?"

There was a group groan.

"If Esmerelda hadn't interfered last night, you would have been my squeaky toy." Lobo snapped.

Alex thought for a moment. "Esmerelda, didn't you say that in all of your lives, you have had a cat that helped you?"

Esmerelda moved to take the empty seat next to Gato. "Yes. This is the first lifetime I haven't had a cat. Why?"

Alex looked at Diego. Once Diego's eyes met his, he looked over at Gato. Diego followed his eyes. Diego's eyes went wide. "Do you think?"

"Well, it makes sense," Alex answered.

Feeling uncomfortable with their stares, Gato asked, "Why are you guys staring at me?"

"Oh, my God," Freddy gasped.

Esmerelda looked at the three of them. "What?"

"How did we miss it?" Lobo asked, shaking his glittering head.

Exasperated, Gato asked again, "What?"

"Your cat," Alex pointed at Gato, "is Gato."

Esmerelda looked at Gato. She studied him, then covered her mouth when she said, "Oh, my goddess."

"I'm not a cat," Gato defended.

"Dude," Freddy leaned forward. "Your name literally is cat. You've protected her since you met her."

Gato reiterated, "I'm not a cat."

"In this life," Esmerelda said solemnly. "I think we just need to awaken your memories."

Angrily, Gato stood up and shouted, "I'm not a cat!"

Standing as well, Esmerelda said, "Gato."

When Gato turned to face her, she pressed her lips to his. Gato was shocked at first, but then kissed her back. Deepening the kiss, he put his arms around her. Esmerelda pulled him close.

The intricate tattoos on Gato's arms glowed and became more vibrant before fading back to normal. In the tattoos, tiny cat eyes popped up. Various cats, from the cunning housecat to the king of the beast lion, started roaming around Gato's arm.

Ending the kiss, Gato put his forehead against Esmerelda's. He softly said, "Mi Gitana."

"What is all this noise?" Juan Carlos asked, stepping back into the room with an arm around Aaron's waist.

Excitedly, Diego said, "Gato is a cat!"

Juan Carlos shook his head in dismay. "Very good, Diego. Gato is cat and perro is dog. Why are you giving me a Spanish lesson?"

"I'm not. Gato," Diego pointed at the man, "is a cat. Esmerelda's cat, to be specific."

Aaron turned around, saying, "I need another drink."

"Can we, please, hold off on any more magic until Aaron wraps his head around it, or he will pass out drunk?" Juan Carlos pleaded.

Returning with an almost full rocks glass of brown liquor, Aaron stopped at Juan Carlos's side. "I think I'm good now." He took a healthy sip from the glass. "By the way, you're out of whisky."

"How is this possible?" Esmerelda asked, running her hands up and down Gato's arms.

Gazing at Esmerelda, Gato answered, "I don't know. I know that after my last lifetime, I realized I was in love with you."

"Aww." Diego swooned before asking, "Did Lobo ever chase Gato?" When everyone stared at him, he added, "You know, dog." He pointed to Lobo, then to Gato. "Cat."

"Diego! That's highly insensitive!" Alex reprimanded before sheepishly admitting, "But since he asked, I'd like to know, too."

"Me, too." Juan Carlos added.

Staring down into the drink he was swirling, Aaron said, "It's a legitimate question."

"You guys do realize we're not really a cat and wolf, right?" Lobo asked. "We are mystical beings."

Gato laughed. "I used to chase him. He was so scared of me."

"He used to pounce on me from out of nowhere," Lobo explained. "Let's see how you'd react if a ball of fur randomly jumped on your back and dug its claws in you."

Freddy shouted over the laughter, "Guys! Can we save the stupid questions for another time? We need to find my true love, and Esmerelda needs to banish Don Marcos back to Hell."

"Freddy is right. Everyone, let's sit down and get serious about this." Juan Carlos put a hand on Aaron's shoulder. "Are you going to be okay with all this?"

Aaron took a sip of his drink. "I don't really have a choice now, do I?"

Once everyone took their seats around the living room, Juan Carlos began, "Let's review what we do know. We're looking for a man named Salvador that went to a bar that Esmerelda, Freddy, and Lobo are banned from."

"I also know that Don Marcos's prison is here, and some rat-faced boy bought it at auction. What was his name?" Esmerelda pulled out her phone and began tapping away. "I was able to get the buyer's list from the auction house. Here it is. Finn Andrews."

"Finn Andrews?!" Diego exclaimed. "Daniel Andrews's son?"

Esmerelda studied her phone. "Yes, I believe that is his father."

"I'll call his father up and negotiate for the orb," Juan Carlos said simply.

"Um," Diego raised a hand. "About that. He wouldn't sign the contract because you weren't there and wanted us to compensate him for that and then threatened to double the price. Let's just say he didn't leave happy."

"Is there anything else I should know?" Juan Carlos groaned.

Diego cringed. "Dion isn't our secretary anymore."

"What?!" Juan Carlos nearly jumped out of his seat. "What did you do?"

"I promoted her," Diego answered sheepishly.

Juan Carlos relaxed. "Oh, well, you should have said that. Alex, please smack your boyfriend in the head for me."

"No," Alex answered, then asked, "Okay, if you guys can't go to this bar, what if one of us goes? We could go tonight."

Freddy shook his head. "Tonight is Monday. Only magical beings are allowed in."

"Don't think you can bribe or push your way through," Esmerelda added. "The demigod Hercules works the door, and he has no use for money."

"Why don't we have Diego stake out the bar as Shadow Guardian?" Juan Carlos suggested.

Lobo shook his sparkling head. "It won't work. The In Between is protected by a perception spell."

"It's a spell that lets you see the bar, but you won't really focus on it or anyone coming and going from the bar," Esmerelda explained. She thought for a moment. "I did run into him when he came out of a building. Maybe he lives there."

"Daniel Andrews is probably still in town. He likes to use these trips to indulge his vices." Juan Carlos pulled out his phone. "Freddy, do you think when you feel better that you'd be up for seducing his son?"

Esmerelda and Lobo chuckled.

Freddy whined, "That was Esmerelda's plan. Why does everyone want me to be the honey trap?"

"Because you're the sweetest," Diego teased.

Gato put an arm around Esmerelda. "We also need to find out what it means that I'm not in cat form this lifetime. That's not normal."

The air above the coffee table shimmered. White sparks began popping. A scroll slowly faded into existence. The sparks stopped, and the shimmering stopped. The scroll spun around, then flew over to Esmeralda and dropped in her lap.

"I need a drink." Aaron announced. Before he could take a sip, Juan Carlos took the glass and took a healthy drink before handing back the almost empty glass.

Juan Carlos coughed from the cool burn of the whiskey. "Okay, that was freaky."

Esmerelda opened the scroll and read aloud,

My Gitana,

I have seen to the care of your lost soul and fostered the gift you gave him. I sent him to your city, knowing Fate and Destiny would put each in the other's path.

I may have also redirected the soul rebirth lines for you. You deserve true happiness, as well.

Lastly, seek out Demona Angel. You will need all your allies in the coming battle.

Love,
Madame Zelda

The scroll began to glow brightly. There was a flash of light. The scroll was gone, leaving a golden pendant and sieved knife in Esmerelda's hands. Aaron took a swig of his drink. He handed the almost empty glass to Juan Carlos, who downed the rest.

"My dagger and necklace," Esmerelda said in awe. "I thought they were lost."

Everyone was quiet until Diego asked, "Who is Demona Angel? She sounds like a badass."

CHAPTER 21

D EMONA SET HER PAPERWORK down and watched Salvador cross the room and head behind the bar. She turned her attention to Herc at the front door. He confirmed her suspicion with a nod. Turning her attention to Ryuu behind the bar, her suspicions were further confirmed by the slight glint of his skin when Salvador got near him.

Ryuu's silvery eyes caught hers. She directed him over to Herc with her eyes. She stood and went over to the bar. Salvador was busy getting the bar ready for the night. "Salvador," she said cautiously. "A word, please."

"Sure." Salvador wiped his hands on a bar towel, then leaned over the bar. "If it's about calling Esmerelda, I haven't yet. I'm calling her Wednesday, just like you told me."

Demona gave him a false smile. Now that she was closer, she could really feel his mystic powers. "Good." She started drawing a small circle on the bar with her index finger. "Tell me, Salvador, what brought you to Morgan City?"

"Oh." Baffled, Salvador smiled. "Well, the woman who raised me sent me here."

Looking down at the circle she was tracing, Demona asked, "This woman, did she send you here? To this bar?"

"Yeah, I woke up one morning, and she announced that she was moving on and that I needed to go find my destiny here in Morgan City." Salvador shrugged. "I packed up my things, and off I went."

Demona eyed him suspiciously. "Where did she go?"

"She just said she was moving on. She didn't say where." Salvador thought long and hard before he added, "I don't think she's with us anymore. I do feel her from time to time, guiding me."

Demona mulled the words over. She boldly asked, "What was her name?"

"Madame Zelda." Salvador laughed. "She said she was 'Queen of the Gitanos.'"

Demona stopped running her finger over the bar. She stared intently at Salvador until his smile faded. "Did she send you here? To this bar?"

"No." Salvador thought for a moment. "Maybe she did. I was walking down the street when a flier for this bar came flying at me. On it was written 'open auditions on Saturday nights.'"

Demona tapped her finger on the bar. "Interesting." She thought for a minute. "Nice chat. I need to go over some things with Ryuu and Herc."

"Okay." Salvador returned to his duties.

Joining Ryuu and Herc at the entrance, she said, "I don't think he knows what he is."

"How can he not?" Herc asked in his usual gruff, deep tone. "And how did he get in here two nights in a row without us sensing him?"

Demona looked back at Salvador, working behind the bar. "I think he was shrouded somehow." She looked back at the two men. "We need to keep an eye on him. In and out of the club."

"A pixie or fairy might be able to watch him undetected." Ryuu's nostrils flared, scenting the air with brimstone. "If need be, I know an Elven assassin that can make it look like an accident."

"No!" Demona said harshly. "We are a neutral place, and we must maintain that appearance. If it got out that we had a mystical assassinated, we could lose our charter, and we'd lose our home."

Herc grumbled, "What do we know about him? What's stopping us from ending him for violating the laws of the bar?"

"He was raised by Madame Zelda," Demona answered quietly. "We don't do anything until I talk to Esmerelda." She turned his attention to Ryuu. "Get eyes on him."

Herc cut his eyes toward Salvador. "Madame Zelda has been dead for what? A thousand years? I don't believe him."

"Do you want to risk it if he's not lying?" She followed his eyes to Salvador. "I'll call Esmerelda in a bit. For now, we act as if we don't have a Siren working alongside us."

Esmerelda pulled into a spot in front of her building. Freddy was sleeping soundly in the backseat. She reached over and took Gato's hand in hers. She didn't know how Madame Zelda had been able to bless her with this unimaginable gift, and she wasn't going to ask how or why.

"Are we going to talk about it?" Gato asked

Esmerelda wouldn't meet his eyes when she said, "I don't want to. We shouldn't question this gift from Madame Zelda."

174

"Not that." Gato laughed. "I'm talking about Demona. How are you going to get her to talk to you after what you did?"

Insulted, Esmerelda exclaimed, "What I did?! That chupacabra threatened to claw my face off!"

"You did spill your drink all over them, then tell them that it made their outfit look better." Gato chuckled. "They weren't really going to claw your face off. It was In Between. You didn't have to banish them to a Hell dimension."

Flippantly, Esmerelda said, "I brought them back. How was I supposed to know that chupacabra was Demona's ...? Girlfriend? Boyfriend? What were they?"

"Chupacabra are gender fluid," Freddy groaned from the back. "Can you, please, get me out of the backseat of this sardine can of a car?"

Esmerelda glared back at Freddy from the rearview mirror. "I'm sorry, maybe we should have taken your car; oh, wait, you don't have one."

"You know I can't drive," Freddy grumbled. "Come on, I'm hungry and need to get back to bed."

Gato shook his head in amusement. "You two never change. Lifetime after lifetime." He got out of the car, then helped Freddy get out. "Come on, Freddy."

"I have some leftover arroz con pollo in the refrigerator you can have," Esmerelda announced, shutting her car door.

Guiltily, Freddy looked at her. "I ate that before I went over to Diego's and Juan Carlos's. The chuletas, too."

"The chorizo?" Esmerelda asked with a sigh. The look on Freddy's face told her the answer. "I'll order a pizza."

Gato helped Freddy around the car. "Make that two. I would like a slice too."

"I'll make it three." Esmerelda pulled out her phone. Before she could dial the number of a local pizzeria, she had an incoming call from the last person she expected. "Why is Demona calling me?" Then the phone was knocked from her hand when two strong arms grabbed her.

Finn had intended to wait until tomorrow to trace the magical trails of Don Marcos's curse, but the strange pulses along the lines of magic sent gut-wrenching pains through him. No sooner had the first subsided when the second magical quake surged forth. He had no choice but to investigate before the magical tremors left him drained and helpless.

Summoning the men he had chosen earlier, Finn kissed his foolish fiancé goodbye and headed out to follow the magic trail. The first line he followed led him back to the city and to the bar run by the half-breed. He knew there was no way he could retrieve whichever cursed soul was there.

The second trail of magic led Finn and his mindless muscle minions toward the less desirable part of town. Finn narrowed his eyes at the tiny sports car driving in front of them. He could feel the tug on his power coming from it. He mentally instructed the driver to follow them.

They pulled into a spot several spaces behind where the sports car had parked. Finn leaned forward from the back seat, eager to see the occupants of the vehicle. Finn sensed magic in the first man with arms covered in tattoos that got out, but not the magical tether. The man he helped out was the one pulling on Finn's magic. Then a woman stepped out of the driver's side.

"It's that bitch from the auction." Finn's eyes glowed red with anger. "She must be the Gitana." Leaning back in the seat, he mentally commanded his muscle minions, <Capture them.>

Wordlessly, the men exited the SUV. Finn watched with intrigue as the men marched over. Finn's soon-to-be prisoners were too busy talking amongst themselves to notice the pretty muscle men approaching, and they had yet to sense him so close.

Your arrogance shall be your downfall, just like Don Marcos. Finn laughed to himself.

They didn't see the four men until it was too late. One of the men grabbed the Gitana from behind, sending her phone crashing into the ground. Using the element of surprise, one of the other men snatched the weakened man from the tattooed man. The tattooed man reacted quickly, easily fending off his two assailants.

Finn watched the tattooed man with fascination. A fist landed on the jaw of one man. A roundhouse kick to the other. After a quick uppercut to the first man, he leaped up into the air, landing with the gracefulness of a cat behind the man holding the tethered man. He clapped the muscle minion's ears, disorienting him.

The weakened man slammed his head back into the face of his captor. The muscle minion released his prisoner to cover his blood-gushing nose. The weakened man, having gotten some surge of strength from somewhere, picked the bleeding muscle minion up and hurled him into the other two muscle minions that were charging at them. With three of his muscle minions dealt with, they turned to help the Gitana.

She did not need their help. Finn felt it. The power she drew upon was almost limitless. He knew he was no match for her at his current strength. He needed to get bonded with Dante and boost his power if he wanted any kind of chance of defeating her. For now, he had to rely on his cunning.

Finn saw the sparks of red and purple magical sparks from the Gitana's fingertips. Magic swirled up along her arms, then around her body. She glowed for an instant. Then the muscle minion that was holding her was sent hurtling back into the wall of the building.

Having dealt with his muscle minions, Finn saw that the three were poised, ready for another attack. He decided to see exactly what he was up against by giving them exactly what they wanted. He sent rejuvenating energy through his connections to the muscle men, healing their wounds and pumping them with some extra power.

His minions lifted themselves up off the ground and moved to surround the three. The one with the magical tether stumbled, and the Gitana caught him. The tattooed man put himself between Finn's muscle minions and his friends. His tattoos began to glow. Four different magical creatures jumped from his illuminated tattoos.

They landed in a protective circle around the Gitana and her friends. Four felines stood ready to defend: a black jaguar, a mountain lion, a puma, and a tiny orange house cat. With their hackles raised and teeth bared, they looked ready and willing to fight anyone trying to breach their circle, with deadly consequences.

Realizing that they could trace his muscle minions back to his luxurious lair if they were caught or killed, Finn mentally commanded them to stop. *Now that I know what they can do, I guess it's time I revealed myself.* Putting on his fakest smile, Finn stepped out of the black SUV.

Addressing the three, Finn called out, "Greetings, Gitana and friends!" Finn strolled casually toward the confrontation. "I apologize for my muscle minions. They didn't quite understand what I meant when I asked them to bring you to me." Finn twirled his hand around in the air. "To me, boys!"

"What are you?" Esmerelda asked, watching their attackers form around him. "And how do you know who I am?"

Finn let out a hearty laugh. "Do you not recognize the lowly rat that guarded Don Marcos's prison?"

"Freddy, let me handle this." She ordered the growling man she was holding up. "Give us Don Marcos, and we'll forgive this attack."

Finn gave her a regretful look. "I wish I could, but I banished him back to Hell." He held out the now-drained honey-amber orb that hung around his neck. "See? Empty."

"Then why hasn't the curse ended?" Freddy snapped.

Finn pretended to fain ignorance. "I would like to know as well. I somehow inherited ownership of the curse when I banished him." Finn sneered at them. "It's an annoying constant itch that I want gone."

"Then help us end it," Esmerelda responded.

"Join forces with you?" Finn pretended to ponder the idea. "I will consider it. Shall we discuss this alliance on neutral ground?"

The tattooed man narrowed his eyes at Finn. "Where?"

"In Between," Finn answered. "Say tomorrow at eight?"

Esmerelda relaxed her stance. "We'll be there."

"Good." Finn snapped his fingers. "Boys, let's go home."

Finn and his muscle minions turned and returned to the SUV, leaving the three still prepared to fight. Pulling away from the battle scene,

Finn toyed with the amber orb hanging around his neck. He let out a fiendish laugh. *Once I'm bonded with Dante, I will end them all.*

CHAPTER 22

J UAN CARLOS PUT AN ARM AROUND
Aaron as he sat down on the couch. Aaron was still shaken up over the earlier events. Juan Carlos had to admit that he, too, was shaken a bit by the appearance of a glittery wolf-like creature sitting on his couch and the sudden appearance of the message for Esmerelda. It was one thing to hear of such things, but to witness them was completely different.

Juan Carlos smiled at Diego and Alex on the other couch playing on their phones, before asking Aaron, "How are you doing?"

"It was a lot to take in." Aaron leaned into Juan Carlos. "Magic. Vigilantes. Creatures from the moon. A man that was a cat in a previous life. Demon."

"I knew all of it, but to actually see it in person." Juan Carlos shook his head.

Diego looked up from his phone. "You've never seen Esmerelda do magic or Freddy change?"

"I've seen Esmerelda do tricks, simple things like lift small objects or summon gusts of wind. As for Freddy," Juan Carlos shrugged, "it just seemed rude to ask to see him change. A little perverted, too."

"Why didn't you tell me about Esmerelda or Freddy? Did you know about Gato?"

Juan Carlos looked at Diego incredulously. "Are you serious? You've called Esmerelda a witch for as long as I can remember. I can't imagine what you would have called Freddy. Gato was as big a shock for me as it was for everyone else."

"I wouldn't have called Freddy anything." Diego grinned. "He might have bitten me."

"Diego," Alex groaned.

Diego pulled Alex into a hug and kissed him on the cheek. "Okay, okay. At least this explains how Freddy was able to lift your heavy planters like they were nothing, but why couldn't he touch the soil?"

"He would have poisoned the soil for the plants with his touch," Juan Carlos explained. "She needs that plant to make a special tea to calm the wolf, err, Lobo, down as the new moon approaches. He apparently gets riled up then."

"That is sad, though." Aaron snuggled close to Juan Carlos. "Being torn away from your home. Then being trapped here where you're forced to look up at the home you can't get back to."

Alex pulled Diego close. "And Freddy, cursed to live life after life, looking for a love that calls out to him, but he can't ever find."

"At least now they have a lead on finding him." Juan Carlos sighed. "Tomorrow, I have to make nice with Daniel Andrews so I can try and convince him to sell us that orb his demon twink son bought."

Diego started scrolling through his phone again. "His son was odd yesterday. He yelled at his father during the meeting. Oh, and when he shook hands with Dion and me, he got this strange look on his face."

"Speaking of Dion. I was thinking about that promotion you offered her." Juan Carlos looked at Aaron and then at Diego. "I was thinking that she should take my job. That way, I can step back and pursue some other interests."

Diego put down his phone. "You want to leave the company? You can't! I need you!"

"Diego, you'll always have me. I just," Juan Carlos kissed Aaron on the cheek, "want to start really living my life and start pursuing some of my passions."

As much as Diego wanted to argue with Juan Carlos about his decision, he couldn't. "I understand, but I still want you as a consultant for special projects."

"Okay," Juan Carlos conceded. "I'll also train Alex to run the Shadow Guardian command center."

Aaron stiffened. "Can we pretend I don't know about the whole Shadow Guardian thing?"

"Of course, mi amor." Juan Carlos rubbed Arron's shoulder soothingly. "If it upsets you, we'll just—"

"It doesn't upset me." Aaron cut him off. He stood and paced the floor. "I'm considering running for police chief."

Juan Carlos jumped up and hugged Aaron. "That's wonderful! We can help you get the support of the Northside!"

Aaron reluctantly hugged Juan Carlos back. "I really haven't decided yet. A young man that wants to challenge Mayor Trainer in the next election approached me about running as a joint ticket."

"We definitely need new leadership in this city," Diego commented. "Who is this young man?"

"Felipe Montoya," Aaron answered.

Juan Carlos's brow furrowed in thought. "Why do I feel like I should know that name?"

"Can we worry about it tomorrow?" Diego asked. "We have more important matters to discuss."

Alex cocked his head at Diego. "Like what?"

"Freddy's party, obviously," Diego answered. "Now that we know about Lobo, we can have a party for him now."

Alex shook his head. "Diego, you know the new moon is on his birthday, and that's why he's not having a party. He goes to the woods and lets Lobo howl out his sorrow."

"We could have it the day before," Diego suggested, a mischievous grin spreading across his face. "I've picked out so many great presents for them, and a couple for Gato, too!"

Aaron looked at Diego, then at Juan Carlos. "You don't need to be a detective to see he's way too excited about that."

"Diego," Juan Carlos said suspiciously. "What kind of presents?"

Diego chuckled guiltily. "Just some things I thought they might like."

"Let me see your phone." Alex snatched his phone from his hand and began reading aloud. "An assortment of squeaky toys, doggy treats, a Frisbee, tennis balls, and a flea collar."

Juan Carlos groaned. "Diego."

"What did he order for Gato?" Aaron asked, laughing.

"Catnip, a toy mouse, and," Alex paused, trying not to laugh, "kitty litter."

Juan Carlos asked sarcastically, "What, no laser pointer?"

"Add that to the list!" Diego exclaimed excitedly.

Alex handed Diego back his phone. "No."

"Diego, if you give them those presents, they are going to kick your ass," Juan Carlos warned. "And I'm not going to stop them."

CHAPTER 23

AFTER HIS ENCOUNTER WITH THE Gitana and her crew, Finn knew he needed to prepare if he wanted to survive his next encounter with them. He hoped that they believed he was sincere about meeting to discuss an alliance. It would buy him time until he secured Dante as his partner and supercharged himself from the throngs of virile young men in the building.

In the meantime, he needed to conserve what power he had. That meant he needed to end the minor curse on his genetic father. With a snap of his fingers, he solved that problem. He wouldn't admit it, but he didn't want the man to suffer. It was quick and painless. The man's heart just simply stopped.

Tomorrow, he'd call the hotel as a worried son and have them check on him. He would pretend to be the distraught son, and before the ink dried on the death certificate, he'd be the head of Andrews Incorporated. With those resources at his disposal, he'd be able to end the Gitana and her magical misfits.

"Aww, home," Finn murmured softly as they pulled into the building's underground parking. He felt the carnal energies flowing into him almost as soon as they entered. "Clean yourselves up and get some rest." He ordered his muscle minions once they were parked. "Tomorrow, we track down the other one."

Wordlessly, the men exited the vehicle to obey their orders. "I need to find better servants," Finn grumbled as he headed to the elevator. "At least I can rely on Dante."

Cautiously, Finn stepped into the penthouse apartment. Something was off. It wasn't visible to the naked eye, but Finn could feel it. There was a strange magic in the air. His sex servants were gone, and Dante was nowhere to be seen. He worried that the Gitana had somehow found his secret lair.

Slowly gathering his magic, Finn moved around the apartment. He noticed there was something off with his power. It felt like it wasn't truly his, that it wasn't bonded to him as it should be. Before he could reach out and investigate, the feeling subsided.

"You're home!" Finn jumped when Dante's arms surrounded him. "Were you successful?"

Finn relaxed into Dante as the soothing pulses of carnal energy pulsed into him. "No." Finn turned in Dante's lanky arms to face him. "There's been a change of plans."

"What do I need to do?" Dante's eagerness pleased Finn.

Finn started with the most important fact first. "I killed my father."

"Oh! Did you draw it out?! Did he scream in horrific pain as the life left his body?!" Dante asked excitedly.

Fearing disappointment, Finn lied, "Yes."

"Don't lie to me!" Dante roughly pushed him away. "Don't you ever lie to me!"

Finn didn't know why he was explaining himself, other than he was shocked at the outburst. "We couldn't afford any delays if they started asking questions. With a simple heart attack, the company seamlessly passes over to me. If any question arises, the vice presidents can secure their own lap dog until I'm cleared."

"I knew there was a reason I loved you." Dante grabbed Finn by the shirt and pulled him into a kiss. "Again, what do you need me to do?"

Finn found himself a bit turned on and frightened by Dante. "In a few hours, I'm going to follow the weaker magical trail back to its home. Once I know where the person lives, you'll come back with the muscle minions and kidnap him while I play the grieving son."

"That way, it can't be tied to you, but what about me?" Dante asked suspiciously.

Finn grinned. "You're only there to supervise. You don't even have to get out of the car."

"Then I'll pick up the rings so I'm seen across town!" Dante added excitedly.

Finn found himself growing uncharacteristically fond of Dante. "After we're married, I want you to head to Bowenville and take charge of the company. Those vice presidents are stupid, but they are also ambitious. As my husband and legal heir, you'll have full authority."

"Mm, power." Dante purred seductively.

CHAPTER 24

"**F**REDDY IS SLEEPING," ESMERELDA announced as she returned to the living room. "I can't believe they broke my phone." She sat down on the couch next to Gato. "Demona was calling me when they attacked."

Gato pulled out his phone. "Use mine."

"I can't." Esmerelda pushed his phone back at him. "She has an enchanted number. If she doesn't put it in your phone, you can't call it."

Tucking his phone away, Gato suggested, "One of us could go down there."

"It's mystical Monday. Even if I could get in, the place will be packed." Esmerelda slumped into the couch.

Gato reached over and took her hand in his. "So, can we talk about that night?"

"I'd rather not, but I guess we should." Giving Gato's hand a squeeze, Esmerelda closed her eyes. "I shouldn't have been cocky and tried to walk home alone that night. I should have let you walk me home."

Gato brought her hand to his lips for a kiss. "I shouldn't have been so forward with you; otherwise, you would have."

"Your machismo had nothing to do with it." Esmerelda laughed. "I found it endearing, you strutting around like a peacock trying to get my attention."

Gato grinned. "Do you know how many favors I did for Juan Carlos for him to talk to you on my behalf?"

"More than you should have." Esmerelda looked at Gato with watery eyes. "If you hadn't followed me home that night, I wouldn't be here. I should have heard him coming up behind me."

Gato moved to hold her. "I saw him knock you down, and then he was standing over you with that pipe about to hit you. He was calling you names." Gato paused. "I just acted."

"I looked over and saw you on top of him punching." Esmerelda laid her head on his chest. "If I hadn't stopped you..." Esmerelda let the sentence hang.

Gato hugged her tight. "I would have killed him."

"Gato, how can you forgive me so easily?" Esmerelda asked in a choked sob.

Gato lifted her head so he could look her in the eyes. "It's what I've done every lifetime since we met. Protect you."

"But your family?" Esmerelda asked, her lip quivering.

Gato wiped away a stray tear that ran down her cheek. "Juan Carlos and Diego have them set up in a nice place in Bowenville. They set up an education fund for them, too, not just the kids. My mother got her GED and is going to school to be a social worker."

"But—"

Gato cut her off. "No buts. While I was in prison, I met men like me with extreme sentences. More than a few are innocent. Now that I'm out here, I want to help them."

Esmerelda began tracing the lines of Gato's tattoos with her finger. "I just wish there was a way for me to make it up to you."

"How about another kiss?" Gato asked smoothly.

With a coy smile, she said, "That I can do."

CHAPTER 25

S HAKING HER HEAD FERVENTLY, Dion proclaimed, "No!"

"Diego and I already discussed it," Juan Carlos explained. "If you don't take the position, someone else will have to. I'm stepping down."

Dion shifted uneasily in her chair. "I could never replace you."

"We don't expect you to. We want you in the position, not Juan Carlos 2.0," Juan Carlos explained. "You already know how to do ninety percent of my job. The other ten percent is working with Diego, and I'll be around to help out with that."

Dion leaned forward. "He had me strip down to my underwear so Alex could spray us down with an experimental bio-suit for the Andrews meeting."

"You did it, though." A smirk crossed Juan Carlos's face. "You didn't want to touch that brat's snot-covered hand."

"True." Dion sat back in the chair. "The thing is, what if what happened with Daniel Andrews happens with another of our suppliers or customers? He would only work with you."

Juan Carlos gestured the comment away with his hand. "He was trying to intimidate you to get a better deal, and it backfired on him. The only chemical we can't get elsewhere easily is one of the key components for Build and Burn, and we don't make that anymore."

"But—"

"No, buts!" Juan Carlos exclaimed. "What is with everyone and these *buts*? I have confidence in you. Diego has confidence in you. Now, you need to have confidence in yourself."

Dion sat there quietly for a moment. She straightened in her seat. Looking Juan Carlos in the eye, she asked, "When do I start?"

"As soon as you find your replacement," Juan Carlos said proudly.

Dion corrected him, "Replacements. I was pulling double duty as your and Diego's personal assistant, remember? No one wanted the job after Diego nearly set the last one on fire."

"That was an accident," Juan Carlos defended. "She unexpectedly walked in right as Diego was testing a prototype blowtorch."

Dion looked at Juan Carlos incredulously. "The flame was three feet long."

"Why do you think we scrapped it?" Juan Carlos shrugged.

"Mamacita," Diego buzzed in. "Are you free?"

Juan Carlos looked at Dion. She gave him a nod. "Yes."

"Can you meet me in my office? Esmerelda's here."

Juan Carlos rushed out of the private elevator into Diego's office. "Esmerelda, is everything okay? How's Freddy?"

"Freddy's fine except that he's eating me out of house and home." Esmerelda greeted him with a kiss on both cheeks. "Gato's with him. As for everything being okay, that depends on how you look at it."

"They were attacked last night," Diego announced.

Juan Carlos stared wide-eyed at Esmerelda. "What? Who? Where?"

"Sit. I'll explain everything." Esmerelda guided him over to one of the chairs. "Before you ask, no one except those muscled brutes was hurt."

"Tell him who it was," Diego growled.

"Silencio." Esmerelda moved her hand in an arc at Diego. "This is my story, not yours."

Diego opened his mouth, but his words had no sound. He tried again and again before grabbing a nearby tablet and typing away. He held up the screen to the two so that they could see the words [Not funny] written on the screen.

"Esmerelda," Juan Carlos said sternly. "You need to teach me that trick." Diego tapped loudly on the words on the screen for emphasis. "Yes, yes. She'll give you back your voice in a minute. Go on, Esmerelda."

Diego slumped back in his chair and began going through his emails. His eyes grew wide when he read the latest email from Dion. He fruitlessly started waving his hands frantically at the two to try to get their attention.

Ignoring Diego's antics, Esmerelda said, "Apparently, Gato wasn't the only one given a human body this go around. Don Marcos's little rat servant was also reborn into a human body. He claims to have banished Don Marcos to Hell and thinks he's Don Marcos's demon heir or something."

"What are we going to do?" A crumpled piece of paper hit Juan Carlos. He looked at Diego, who was frantically pointing at his computer screen. "Diego! Stop playing around!" Turning his attention back to Esmerelda, he said, "I can still reach out to Daniel Andrews and see if he can help."

Getting an idea, Diego straightened in his chair and began frantically typing at his computer.

Esmerelda shook her head. "This is out of his hands now. The boy definitely has some sort of power. He showed up with these enthralled muscle men." Esmerelda thought for a moment. "It's weird. I sensed power in him, but it didn't seem like it was his. He's definitely a demon, and he definitely has taken ownership of the curse. If I were to guess, I'd say he's a lower-class demon at best."

"And he was foolish enough to attack you?" Juan Carlos asked in disbelief

"He claims his brutes misinterpreted his orders to bring us to him." Esmerelda smiled. "We took care of them easily enough."

Juan Carlos leaned back in his chair. "What's the plan?"

"He asked to meet on neutral ground to discuss a possible truce to end the curse. We're meeting him at In Between tonight." Esmeralda sighed. "I wish I could call Demona and let her know I'm coming. My phone was damaged in the fight."

Juan Carlos held out his phone. "Use mine."

"It's an enchanted number," Esmerelda explained. "I dropped my phone off with Alex, hoping he could fix it."

Juan Carlos thought for a moment. "Can't you send a magical note like the one we got last night?"

"I wish. The place is enchanted. I would have sent a magical courier, but most of the mystical beings won't have anything to do with me." Esmeralda sighed. "You banish one gender-fluid chupacabra to a Hell dimension in a previous life, and you never live it down."

There was a knock on the door. Juan Carlos and Esmerelda looked at Diego to answer. Remembering Diego's predicament, Juan Carlos shouted, "Come in!"

"Hey, Esmerelda, I got your screen fixed," Alex announced, opening the door. Handing her phone back to her, he said, "It was a simple screen replacement. The one I put on isn't factory, but it's nearly indestructible."

"Thank you." Esmeralda scrolled through her phone. "Damn, the number isn't there. The enchantment broke with the screen."

Alex gave Diego a queer look. "Diego, why are you waving your hands at me?"

"Hey, guys." Dion stepped into the office behind Alex. "Why did Diego send me a message titled [Ultra critically urgent! Do this right now!] followed by like a hundred exclamation points to come in here and tell you that Daniel Andrews was found dead in his hotel room this morning?"

Esmerelda waved her hand in an arc and said, "Habla."

"Thank you." Diego glowered at Esmerelda. "Thank you, too, Dion."

Dion shook her head. "Things just get weirder and weirder around here."

"You have no idea," Alex responded.

"Alright, how do we take down that demon twink if he betrays you?" Diego asked.

Dion threw her arms up in the air. "I'm out. I don't know what's going on, and I don't want to."

CHAPTER 26

IT WAS NEARLY EIGHT AT NIGHT before Finn's car pulled into the garage of the apartment complex. He had spent hours dealing with the fallout of his human father's death. Finn couldn't believe these creatures had made such a simple thing like death so complicated. It was draining to pretend to be upset and sad while people gave their false sympathies.

Things were much simpler in the nether realms. There was no paperwork that needed to be signed and notarized. There was no statement that needed to be given or verification of death. When a demon was vanquished, everyone scrambled to claim their possessions and moved up the pecking order.

Fortunately, Dante's "daddy" was able to help speed the process along. It left a bad taste in Finn's mouth knowing that the mysterious "daddy" helped him, but it had freed his day up to go to one of the satellite offices of Andrew Incorporated to formally take charge of the company before any of those backstabbing idiot vice presidents had a chance to act.

The one thing he didn't have to worry about was capturing the other person pulling on his magic. Dante had texted him shortly after Finn arrived at the hotel that they had him bound and gagged in the back of the SUV. That meant he had one less errand to do. He just had to send one of his muscle minions over to In Between with a note.

Why am I so weak? Finn pondered. He was leaning on a blonde muscle minion for support to get to the elevator. He'd noticed his energy levels growing dangerously low as the day went on. At one point, he had felt his connections to his thralls falter, and he could feel the magical trails of the curse, but he couldn't follow them.

By the time they reached the penthouse apartment, Finn was being carried like a feeble baby by the muscle minion. It was as disturbing as it was embarrassing. *Did the Gitana curse me somehow?* Finn wondered. He could barely keep his eyes open. Fortunately, Dante was there to ensure he was taken care of.

"Take him to the bedroom." Finn heard Dante order the minion. "Be quick about it."

A few moments later, Finn felt the soft press of a bed under him. "Don't worry. I'll take care of you, baby." Dante's wet warm lips pressed to his. There was a slight trickle of power that eased Finn's exhaustion. "You just lay there, and I'll take care of you."

Finn struggled to open his eyes. "Did you get the rings?"

"Of course I did." Dante caressed his cheek. "I also have that creature you wanted, gagged and bound in the other bedroom with several guards."

Finn smiled weakly. "Good. After we're married and you're on your way to Bowenville, I'll return here and set my trap for the Gitana and her friends."

"What are you going to do?" Dante asked, playing with Finn's hair.

Finn felt almost normal now. "There's a special ritual that will sever his tie to this plane of existence so that when he dies, he won't be reborn back into this world."

"I'm guessing he's going to have an unfortunate accident after." Dante laughed. "Wait, didn't you have a meeting tonight?"

Finn pulled Dante on top of him. "I sent my regrets for not being able to make the meeting with one of my minions." Finn kissed Dante. A spark of energy surged into him. "Since we can't have our honeymoon after our wedding, why don't we have it before?"

"Mm, yes, sir," Dante purred.

CHAPTER 27

"**I** CANNOT BELIEVE YOU EMBAR-
rassed me like that," Esmerelda chastised.
Diego looked at her with a confused look.
"What? That was Hercules. Like the real Hercules
from all those Greek myths and stuff?" Diego
stopped to look back at the doorman, then asked,
"That was the Hercules, right? I don't remember
the stories saying he was black."

"Yes, that was the real Hercules. The Greeks
changed how he looked in their stories." Freddy
laughed, putting an arm around Diego's shoulder.
"Whatever you do, don't ask him to wrestle. He
does it the old Greek style."

Diego grinned. "That might be fun."

"I don't think Alex will approve." Gato
motioned everyone into a booth. "You all wait
here. I'll go make nice with Demona."

"You have a lot of nerve coming into my bar after what you did, Esmerelda." Demona popped up beside Gato.

Freddy groaned, "Too late."

"We're here on official business. Once it's done, we'll leave," Esmerelda said curtly. "I would have called, but my phone was damaged. Would you mind putting your number back in for me?" Fluttering her eyelashes, Esmerelda held out her phone. "Please?"

Demona waved her hand over the screen. "There, now I want to know why you sent a Siren in here with one of your cards." Demona glowered. "I also want to know how you hid what he was from us."

"You sent a Siren in here?" Gato asked, wide-eyed.

Diego grew excited. "Wait, there are sirens, too? Oh, please, tell me there are dragons, and I can meet one."

"He's at the bar." Demona nodded over to Ryuu. "You look like his type." Demona paused. "To eat."

Esmerelda thought for a moment. "I didn't give my card to a Siren. The only person I gave my card to was Salvador, the guy I bumped into."

"Yes, him." Demona crossed her arms. "Now, how did you hide what he was from us? You know the rules of In Between."

Esmerelda thought for a moment. "Madame Zelda."

"Wait, my beloved is a Siren?" Freddy asked. "How is that possible?

Diego slipped out of the booth. "Do I look good enough to meet a dragon?"

"Guys!" Gato shouted over everyone. "Demona, Esmerelda didn't send a Siren into your bar. I don't think he was a full-blown Siren when he came in here. Madame Zelda must have awakened that part of him when she sent the note."

Demona cocked her head at Gato. "Who are you?" It took her a moment to see who Gato really was. "You're human in this life? How?"

"Madame Zelda," Gato answered.

Demona put her head in her hand in thought. "Okay, here's what we're going to do." She flipped a gold coin to Diego. "Pretty boy, you take that and give it to Ryuu. He likes shiny things. The rest of us are going to sort this out."

"I'm not a pretty boy." Diego groused before rushing off to the bar.

Demona slipped into the booth, followed by Gato. "How is it possible for Madame Zelda to be involved? She's been dead for I don't know how many years." Demona shook her head. "Fucking magic."

"She sent me a note telling me that she fostered the gift I gave him." Esmerelda thought for a moment. "How could I have turned him into a Siren? I don't have that kind of power."

"Sing to him," Freddy said softly. "You told Sabastian to sing to me."

Gato reached out and took Esmerelda's hand. "You didn't mean to. You were young and had just gotten your powers."

Freddy looked Demona in the eye. "Do you know where Salvador is?"

"He should be coming in any moment now." Demona looked at her watch. "Funny, he's late. It's past eight."

"Where is that demon twink we're supposed to be meeting?" Esmerelda looked around the empty bar. "If he stood us up." She pounded her fist on the table.

Gato covered her hand with his. "Calm down. There could be traffic. We don't know where he's coming from."

"I know where I'm going to send him. To Hell, if I have any say in it," growled Freddy.

Demona narrowed her eyes at the two. "Not in my bar, he's not."

"I have a message for Esmerelda." Herc dropped a letter on the table. "Some enthralled pretty boy dropped it off."

They were all silent as Esmerelda opened the note. She read aloud to everyone.

Gitana,

I have the one you're looking for, so there's no need for any truce negotiations. Surrender your powers to me, and I'll free him. If you don't, I'll go through with the ritual of separation. Meet me in the abandoned train yard at the edge of town. Come alone.

Esmerelda set the note down. "That rat bastard."

"Ryuu!" Demona yelled. "Stop letting that pretty boy touch your scales and get over here."

Pulling his arm away from Diego, Ryuu jumped up over the bar and landed gently at the table. "What is it, boss?"

"Why didn't your fairy spy tell us that Salvador was kidnapped?" Demona's eyes flared, one red, one white.

Ryuu raised an eyebrow at her. "Because he wasn't."

"We just got a note from the demon twink saying he kidnapped Salvador." Esmerelda glowered.

Ryuu pointed to the door. "Then who is that?"

Everyone turned to see Salvador rushing in the door. He stopped when he saw everyone staring at him. "What?" Then he saw him. The man from his dreams. "It's you."

"It's me." Freddy jumped out of the booth, landing beside Ryuu. "It's you."

"Is that the Siren?" Diego asked, moving to stand next to Ryuu.

It was like they were watching it in slow motion. Salvador dropped his bag and cautiously moved toward Freddy. Freddy mirrored his step, his eyes welling with tears. They both began trembling at the joy of finally finding their true love. Freddy reached out with a hand. Salvador did the same. Right as their fingertips were about to touch, a blazing white light threw them both sailing back from each other.

"What the actual fuck?" Demona groaned.

A blue-tinted white orb floated where Freddy and Salvador were blasted from. Its light pulsed as it spoke. "Salutations. I am Cotto, herald of the Lunaray royal family. I apologize for my dramatic entrance."

"Dramatic?" Diego snipped, going over to help Freddy. "You could have killed them."

"I assure you that was not my intention," Cotto said. "I was trying to prevent the death of Federico and Lobo."

Demona motioned for Herc to tend to Salvador. "What do you mean, 'to prevent the death of Federico and Lobo?'"

The orb pulsed rapidly for a moment before explaining, "We are just as eager to have Lobo back in our kingdom as you all are to have the curse broken. Our mystical priests saw Lobo and Federico dying when the curse was lifted. Over their lifetimes, their souls have been intertwined. They are as much of each other as they are themselves."

"You mean that if I ever get to actually touch my true love, I'll die." Tears fell down his cheek. "Lobo and I both agree, death is much easier than having to live these lifetimes in torture."

Diego pulled Freddy into his arms. "We'll find a way. I promise."

"We already have." Cotto pulsed. "It will be ready soon. In the meantime," Cotto floated over to Demona, "we formally ask for asylum for Salvador."

Demona shook her head. "You can't ask for asylum for Salvador. He's not a Lunaray citizen."

"He does work at the bar," Ryuu pointed out. "And he's mystical. That means he could upset the neutrality of this bar if he does the wrong thing."

Demona huffed, "Fine. He bunks with you."

"Can someone please tell me what's going on?" Salvador asked. He was leaning on Herc for support. His eyes were instantly drawn back over to Freddy, leaning against the far wall.

Demona shook her head in dismay. "Herc, go put a 'closed' sign on the front door. This is going to take a while."

"Okay." Herc turned to leave but then stopped to ask, "If they sent a note saying they have Salvador, and he's here, then who do they have?"

CHAPTER 28

Finn felt unusually powerful when he woke up that morning. He attributed it to the hours of pleasure he and Dante gave each other while the men in the building were fornicating in every nook and cranny available to them. By the time they had all finished, Finn was supercharged with carnal energy.

Now he was standing in Mayor Trainer's office with Dante. They were dressed in form-fitting suits that Dante had picked up for them while he was out getting the rings. He was antsy about being out in public. He had realized a little too late that he should have betrayed the Gitana and her crew after the wedding.

"Do you, Finn Andrews, pledge yourself in mind, body, and soul to Dante Fire in this life and the next? To protect him and serve him for as long as you two are bonded?" Mayor Trainer read blandly.

Finn raised an eyebrow at the choice of words. He looked at Dante, who told him with his facial expressions that he needed to answer. "I do." Finn slipped the gold and silver swirled band on Dante's finger.

"Do you, Dante Fire, take Finn Andrews in mind, body, and soul in this life and the next? To take his protection and servitude for as long as you two are bonded?" Mayor Trainer read blandly.

Before Finn could say something about the words he used, Dante said, "I do." Dante slipped an identical band on Finn's finger.

"By the power vested in me, I now pronounce you husband and husband." Mayor Trainer closed the book he was reading from. "You may seal the bond with a kiss."

Dante pulled Finn into a kiss. "Can you believe we're married?!" He asked excitedly. "I can't wait to tell the world!"

"Tell my vice presidents first." Finn pulled Dante back into the kiss. He felt his power surge unexpectedly. "Go. Once I'm done here, I'll join you, and we'll have a real honeymoon."

"Don't worry, baby. I'll put those grumpy old men in their place for you." Dante turned to Mayor Trainer. "Thank you, again, for doing this

for us. It means the world to me that you per-
formed the ceremony."

"You can thank me when it comes time to
make your campaign donations. If you'll excuse
me." Mayor Trainer turned his attention to the
hulking black man in a police chief's uniform carrying in a large box. "I have an important meeting
with Police Chief Brutus."

Dante led Finn from the office and out to the
street. Pulling Finn chest to chest with him, Dante
growled, "Don't take long. I want to put our vows
to good use, baby."

"About the vows—" Finn was interrupted with
his phone ringing. "I need to take this." He kissed
Dante. "We'll talk when I get to Bowenville."
Answering the phone, Finn slipped into his dark-
tinted SUV. "Finn Andrews, how can I help you?"

"Finn. It's Juan Carlos." Finn gritted his teeth
at the name. "I got your number from your office."
Finn made a mental note to fire everyone in his
office. "I was just calling to say that I'm so sorry
to hear about your father. He was a good man."

Finn laughed. "No, no, he wasn't, but thank
you for pretending he was."

"I just wanted to offer an olive branch and say
that if you need anything, please, don't hesitate
to call me." Finn grew suspicious of Juan Carlos.

"I'm not just talking about business. I know how hard it is to lose a parent."

Finn bit back his vile retort and instead said, "Thank you. I think I have it covered. Look, I really appreciate you calling, but I just got married, and I'd like to spend some time with my new husband."

"You got married!" Juan Carlos exclaimed excitedly into the phone. "Congratulations! Who is the lucky young man? Where can I send a wedding present?"

Finn bit the inside of his mouth to keep from snipping at Juan Carlos. "Thank you. We don't need anything. Look, I really have to go. Thank you again for calling, Juan Carlos." Finn ended the call before Juan Carlos could say anything else.

Relaxing back in the seat, he mentally commanded the driver to take them home. He needed to prepare for tonight. *Tonight, I will become the most powerful demon in existence, or deal a fatal blow to one of our most hated enemies. Either way, I'll show those bastards in Hell that I'm not the one they should ignore.*

CHAPTER 29

"**D**ID YOU GET IT?" JUAN CARLOS asked Alex when the phone went dead. Alex tapped at his computer, then the wall screen in front of him came to life with a map of the city. A tiny blip moved along the lines. "I did. I was able to piggyback off your call to share his GPS location with us." Alex paused. "Is this legal?"

"He's a demon twink that has a hostage," Juan Carlos responded. "I checked with Aaron, and he said that's not something the police normally handle. He said twinks were more Diego's territory."

Alex looked down at himself. "I'm not a twink."

"Close enough," Juan Carlos chimed back. "Anyways, once you think you have the location of his lair, let Diego and me know. I need to get back to work." Juan Carlos stood. "I have a ton of things to update Dion on before she officially takes office."

Alex called after him, "About things that need an update, can I ask some questions about this project you have me working on?"

Juan Carlos sat back down. "How can I help?"

"What is it?" Alex asked bluntly. "You forbade me from creating a simulation of it, and the more I read the code, the more confused I get. I don't know what it does, so I can't really figure out a way to counteract it."

Juan Carlos thought for a moment. "This does not leave this office, not even to Diego. Understood?" Alex nodded. "I need to hear you say it."

"Understood," Alex said aloud.

Juan Carlos took in a deep, soothing breath. "When Dr. Wyatt, Timmy, and Jimmy broke into the warehouse to steal the chemicals for Build and Burn—" Juan Carlos paused mid thought. "That son of a bitch."

"What?" Alex cocked an eyebrow at him.

"Remind me to tell you after." Juan Carlos shook his head. "Anyways, someone stole a prototype hypnosis machine. Dr. Gingerman developed it and the software to run it, but it worked too well. It wasn't hypnosis. It was mind control. We kept the machine in case Dr. Gingerman could make it work properly, but we destroyed the hard drive with all the code on how to run it."

Alex thought for a moment. "You think someone has the code to make it work?"

"I hope not." Juan Carlos shook his head. "But I'd rather be prepared in case they do."

Alex nodded. "Got it. Now what was that about Build and Burn?"

"Andrews Industries was the only supplier for one of the chemicals. When I gave Esmerelda a sample to test, she said there was something unnatural about it, but she couldn't figure out what."

Alex said softly, "The demon twink."

"The demon twink." Juan Carlos repeated.

Alex hesitated before asking the next question. "Do you know how Freddy's doing?"

"He's holding up." Juan Carlos smiled. "He may not be able to touch his true love yet, but they can talk and see each other. Esmerelda said they were up for hours video chatting."

Alex smiled. "I'm glad he found Salvador."

"Me, too." Juan Carlos stood.

Alex quickly added, "Juan Carlos?"

"Yes, Alex?" Juan Carlos asked.

Alex gave him a puzzled look. "Why did Diego ask me if I'd be open to a throuple relationship with an asexual dragon? Is that a thing?"

"Apparently so." Juan Carlos shrugged. "Asexual dragons. Demon twinks. Mad bears that destroy the city. Who knows what will be next?"

Alex laughed. "We haven't had Pups yet." Juan Carlos raised an eyebrow at him. "You know, puppy play?"

Juan Carlos began laughing. "Can you imagine that? A bunch of boys running around in puppy masks going, *woof*?"

CHAPTER 30

ENRAGED, FINN BELLOWED AT HIS mindless muscle minions. "Who is this?!" The men looked at each other, not knowing how they should answer, even if they could. "This is not the man I sent you to get!" The men again looked at each other. "Next time I enthrall someone, I'm going to at least let them have some sort of brain." Finn moved to the nearly naked man covered in body glitter chained to the bed. With a quick motion, he ripped the duct tape from the man's mouth.

"Ouch!" The man yelled. "Totally not cool, man. Also, not cool about kidnapping me and stuff, but I dig your bondage kink."

Finn closed his eyes and counted to ten. Opening his eyes, he asked as nicely as he could,

"Who are you? Why are you chained up in my guest bed?"

"Dude, I have no idea why I'm chained up in your guest bed." The man looked over at one of the men. "I'm normally down for this kind of stuff, but I like to, you know, get to know a person before I let them tie me up and stuff."

Finn shook with anger. "Fine. Who are you?"

"Oh, me?" The man chuckled. "I'm Jase. I'm a fairy."

Finn's eyes grew wide with anger. He started shouting at his muscle minions. "You brought me a fucking fairy?! A fucking fairy?!"

"Dude, chill," Jase commented. "It's all good. Just let me go, and I'll be on my way. No harm, no foul."

Finn laughed maniacally. "No harm? No foul? Do you know who your queen is? Do you?"

"Yeah, Rodney is a bit of a bitch when it comes to matters of kidnapping and stuff." Jase thought for a second. "It's kind of odd he's a queen and not a king, right? It's not just me, right?"

Finn shook his head. "I don't care. He can call himself the muffin man for all I care. I just know that if he finds out that I kidnapped you, this place will be overrun with fairy guardsmen." Finn thought for a moment. He smiled at the formation of an idea in his head. "So we'll make sure he doesn't find out. I'll simply take you with me when I leave. Fairies make good pets, don't they?"

"Uh, no," Jase answered. "Our wings wither up and die if we're caged too long. Then our magic slowly leaks away until we're nothing."

Finn taped Jase's mouth shut again. "It's a sacrifice I'm willing to make." He turned his attention to the muscle minions. "Make sure you pack him as well in the morning. I want out of this town at first light." The men nodded. "Oh, and if I'm not back at first light, I want all of you to go rioting in the streets. Don't stop, no matter what. Destroy the city."

CHAPTER 31

"I'M IN POSITION AND HAVE EYES on the penthouse," Shadow Guardian reported from the top of an adjacent building. "It looks like there are two, maybe three men in the penthouse standing around doing nothing. That has to be his hideout. Lobo, what about you?"

A growl came through the radio, "I'm not talking to you."

"Is it because of the squeaky toys?" Shadow Guardian held back a laugh.

Lobo growled again, "Yes."

"Then why did you play with them for ten minutes before we left?" Shadow Guardian asked, not able to hide his amusement.

Lobo sounded a bit happier this time when he said, "Because they squeak."

"Guys, can we please focus?" Alex groaned over the radio. "Gitana? Gato? What about you? Are you in position at the abandoned train yard?"

"Yes." The Gitana answered with a bit of venom in her voice. "If he stands me up this time..."

"I have eyes on him," Gato announced. "I think. There's a black SUV coming down the lane."

"Gato, stay hidden until he makes his move," Alex ordered. "Shadow Guardian, Lobo, be prepared to storm the building. Ryuu said that it's probably the fairy he hired to tail Salvador."

"I'm going to meet a fairy!" Shadow Guardian said excitedly over the com.

Lobo growled, "You'll meet more than you want to if anything bad happens to him. Queen Rodney does not take fondly to one of his own being harmed."

"Remember not to harm the men in the building if you can help it. They are innocents under the demon twink's control," Alex reminded them. "Gitana, we move on your mark," Alex announced.

"He's getting out of the SUV," the Gitana reported. "He's got two of his minions with him." There was a pause. "That asshole. He just took a potshot at me! Go, boys! Go!"

"You heard the lady," Alex shouted across the coms. "Go! Go! Go!"

Shadow Guardian leaped from the building. He deployed his glider wings. The updrafts from the buildings made it hard for him to maneuver. When he was close enough to the building, he retracted his wings and shot out a tendril. It latched on without a problem. He quickly shot another from his other hand to a neighboring building to keep himself from slamming into the wall.

"I'm about three floors from the penthouse," Shadow Guardian reported. He retracted the stabilizing tendril. He moved his body so he could plant his feet against the wall. "I'm climbing up the building now."

"Be careful," Alex said. "Lobo is drawing all the minions down to the lower floors. Drone imagery shows the heat signatures moving down the building."

"Remind him that they aren't squeaky toys," Shadow Guardian huffed, climbing up the side of the building.

A moment later, Alex came back with, "He said fuck you."

"I'm going to miss him." Shadow Guardian laughed. "Only two more floors," He announced. "Let's hope he didn't take the hostage with him or stash him somewhere else." Shadow Guardian shot a new tendril up over the balcony. "You know we should go rock climbing sometime."

"Focus, Shadow Guardian," Alex chided. "And no."

Climbing over the balcony wall, Shadow Guardian crouched low. "Okay, I'm at the penthouse. I see three of those mindless minions. They have their backs to me."

"Use the Shadow darts," Alex ordered. "Those should put them out long enough for you to rescue the fairy."

Shadow Guardian slowly moved across the penthouse balcony. "Got it." He quietly opened the balcony door. He tapped his temple, and Shadow Guardian's targeting computer came up. "Nighty night, fellas." Three darts shot out of Diego's right arm.

Lobo roared at the charging men. They stopped for a moment, looked at each other, then continued their charge. "Are you sure I can't hurt them?" Lobo asked, wanting to extend his claws.

"Only if you have to." Alex came over his earpiece. "Oh, and Shadow Guardian says to remind you that they aren't squeaky toys."

Lobo growled, "Fuck him." He charged the throngs of men, knocking them to the side as he made his path through. "These things aren't that bright, are they?"

"Apparently not," Alex answered. "Esmerelda says that they are basically living zombies."

Lobo swung his left arm, sending several men crashing into the wall. "They just don't stop."

"Just keep them busy until we free the hostage," Alex reminded Lobo. "Once Esmerelda defeats the demon twink, they should stop."

Lobo let out an ear-piercing howl. He picked up a man and tossed him into the crowd of young men attacking him. "They better. They may be stupid, but they have numbers."

"I'll send backup," Alex informed him.

Lobo slammed another two men into the wall with another swipe of his arms. "Backup?" He heard a strange buzzing sound. Then he saw four tiny flying machines hovering over the attacking men. Tiny little darts shot out of the machines at the men. In a matter of seconds, forty or so of the mindless men fell to the ground.

"Backup," Alex said proudly. "I have an idea; see if you can get them to chase you into the underground parking garage."

Lobo snarled, "Lobo doesn't run."

"But he does hunt, right?" Alex asked.

"Gitana, are you okay?" Alex asked.

With a flip of her wrist, the Gitana closed the fan she had used to block the blast. "Yes." She slipped the fan back into its holster. "That little brat is going to pay for that. Gato!"

Wearing just a skin-tight white athletic shirt, Gato strolled out of the shadows to stand beside the Gitana. He clenched his fist to cause the muscles in his arms to bulge. The tattoos on his arms glowed to life. From his arms sprang two black jaguars, a black house cat, and an orange farm cat.

"Let's end this," Gato hissed. Gato took off at a run with the cats. The house cat and farm cat jumped up onto the back of the jaguars, then propelled themselves into the air to latch themselves onto the faces of the two minions. The jaguars tackled the men, pinning them to the ground with their massive paws.

Gato went straight for Finn. Before he could strike, Finn waved his hand and sent Gato hurling away. Gato landed in a crouch on all fours. Magic crackled around Finn's fingertips. He had a red orb of magic in each hand. He sent one hurtling at Gato, the other at the Gitana.

Gato rose up in the air above the flying ball of magic. The Gitana, on the other hand, caught the blast effortlessly and sent it flying back at Finn. He dove out of the way. The blast struck the SUV, sending it up in an explosion of smoke and fire. The Gitana saw the fear on Finn's face, if just for a moment.

Shadow Guardian searched three rooms before he found a glittery, half-naked man chained to the bed. He gripped the side of the duct tape covering the man's mouth. "This is probably going to hurt." He ripped the tape off the man's mouth.

"Fuck, dude." Jase worked his mouth around. "What is with you guys and duct tape? My safe word is pineapple juice, okay? And I'm using it now. Pineapple juice! Pineapple juice! Pineapple juice!"

"Safe word?" Shadow Guardian thought for a moment. "Whoa! Dude! No! I'm here to rescue you. Anything else?"

"Sweet." Jase smiled. "So, are you going to like, magic these chains off me or break them with your super strength?"

Shadow Guardian tapped his temple. "Hey, Alex, did Juan Carlos teach you that chain trick?"

"I'm a little busy here," Alex answered.

"No, I didn't." Juan Carlos came across the line. "Don't worry. I'm here helping Alex. Go on and grab the chain."

"This might tickle." Shadow Guardian put his hand on the cuff holding Jase's left arm. The suit surrounded it, then withdrew a minute or so later, leaving Jase's hand free.

"Awesome." Jase moved his arm around.

Once he had set Jase free, they crept out of the bedroom. "Now we have to fight our way down," Shadow Guardian explained.

"Dude, how did you get up here?" Jase asked.

Shadow Guardian pointed out the balcony. "I came up the wall."

"That's cool." Jase rocked his head back and forth. "You know, I'm like a fairy and have wings, right? I can fly us down."

"Okay, I've got the drones positioned," Alex told Lobo. "Lure them up the ramp."

Lobo howled. "This is fun."

Lobo waited until the twenty or so remaining men gathered together. Once they came charging at him, he ran up the ramp to the next level of the garage. The men followed. Lobo waited at the top of the ramp for them. Once they were running up the ramp, Alex's drones came out of hiding and began firing their Shadow Darts into them.

Lobo let out a triumphant howl. "That's all of them."

"Now, we need to help Shadow Guardian get out with the hostage. Start making..." Alex paused. "Apparently, he got a ride down. Meet him outside."

Lobo chuckled. "He rode the fairy down, didn't he?"

Alex answered through clenched teeth. "Yes."

With Shadow Guardian wrapped in his arms, Jase lowered them down the fifty stories with ease. Landing, Jase's colorful butterfly-like wings disappeared without a trace. Shadow Guardian let go and saw that they had landed in front of Lobo with four of his Shadow Drones hovering about.

"Thanks for the ride." Shadow Guardian stuck out his hand. "I'm sorry, I didn't get your name."

Jase took his hand. "Jase and you are?"

"I'm Shadow Guardian, and these are my friends, Lobo and Shadow Voice," he introduced.

"Cool. Pleasure to meet you guys." Jase withdrew his hand. "I hope you guys don't mind, but I really need to get home. I'm sure my husbands are pissed that I've been gone so long."

Alex's voice came from one of the drones. "No, by all means, go."

"Catch you guys around." Jase's wings appeared again, and he zoomed up and away too fast for them to watch.

Shadow Guardian looked at the drone. "Alex, were you jealous?"

"Shoot him with a dart," Lobo suggested. "I'll say it was an accident."

"We'll talk about it later," Alex huffed through the drone. "Right now, we need to make sure none of those men wake up and leave the building before the Gitana defeats the demon twink."

Gato attacked Finn again, dodging his magical blasts as he prepared to strike. Right before he could land a punch, he found himself tossed across the abandoned lot toward the Gitana. He felt the Gitana's magic catch him and place him gently on his feet beside her.

"We've freed the fairy," Alex's voice buzzed in their ears.

The Gitana put up her arm to stop Gato from attacking again. "He's mine." With her other hand, she touched her medallion. She felt the presence of all the Gitanas before her. Drawing her dagger from its sheath, she walked toward Finn. "You know, we could have found a way to end this curse without me having to banish you back to Hell."

Finn tossed a magical blast at her. With her free hand, she pulled out her fan and clacked it open to block the blast. He was getting weaker. "I'm not sure how you were able to banish Don Marcos to Hell, and I don't care." She blocked another blast, this one the size of a tennis ball.

The Gitana's blade began to glow. "What I do care about is that you tried to hurt me and my family." Finn took an uneasy step back. He tried to send another blast, but only sparks appeared.

"My power!" Finn cried out. "What happened to my power?"

The Gitana was face to face with him now. "You never had any." She snatched the dangling orb from around his neck and crushed it in her palm. She let the dust fly off into the wind. "Tell Don Marcos I said hello." She drove the glowing dagger into Finn's chest.

Finn let out a horrific scream. Like the wolves she had banished so many lifetimes ago, black ooze poured from the wound. Pulling out the dagger, she stepped back to find herself in Gato's arms. They watched as Finn, the demon twink, melted into nothingness, leaving only his clothes behind.

"It's done," Gato said into his earpiece. "We're heading out. Give Aaron the go-ahead to send in the first responders." Gato summoned back his cats. "Are you okay?"

The Gitana looked quizzically at the pile of clothes. "He was so weak. How was he able to enthrall so many men?"

"I don't know," Gato shrugged. "Come on, before the police arrive and we have to explain things we really can't."

CHAPTER 32

FINN WAS FALLING BACK INTO THE bowels of Hell. He prepared himself for the hard slam of his body into the hard rock. Not wanting to watch, he closed his eyes. He'd be the lowest of the low when he got back, but he'd claw and fight his way back up. He'd done it before, and he'd do it again. Then he would exact his revenge on the Gitana and her cohorts.

Finn was surprised that instead of hard bedrock crippling him, he felt a soft cushion catching his body. He opened his eyes to see that he was naked in a round room with no doors or windows, surrounded by large, soft pillows.

Confused, Finn asked aloud, "What happened? Where am I?"

He could hear Dante speaking to someone. "The asset is secured. How goes it on your end?

Good." Dante laughed. "Good, you got the complete set!" Finn looked around to see where Dante's voice came from. "I need to tend to my husband now. Goodbye."

Finn shouted, "Dante!"

"Welcome home, my love." Finn looked around to see where the voice was coming from. "Up here." Finn looked up to see Dante's eye looking down at him. "I'm sorry it happened this way, but it was the best for our long-term plans."

Finn struggled to stand up on the plush cushions. Looking up at Dante, he yelled, "Dante! How did I get in here?!"

"There's no need to shout." Dante laughed. "You see, my dear Finn, you foolishly thought I was some sort of amplifier for your power. That's why you fell so easily into my trap. I'm actually an incubus. That's how I was able to drain you without you realizing it."

Feeling completely exposed, Finn brought his knees to his chest. "Why me?"

"You were the sexy little thing that got in my way," Dante answered. "I was after Don Marcos. You got to him first."

Finn's voice quivered when he asked, "Why didn't you just try to take it from me, then? Why did you let me go through all that with the Gitana?"

"That was the plan, to take it from you," Dante answered. "The problem was you were just too cute!" Finn glowered up at him. "There was also that annoying curse tethered to his powers. By leaving it tethered to you, I was able to go unnoticed. All the benefits and none of the risks!"

"So, I was nothing more than a patsy! A scapegoat!" Finn spat out. "Is that why you brought me here? To gloat! For that matter, how did you bring me here?!"

Dante's voice went saccharine sweet. "Do you not remember our vows? Or exchanging rings made with enchanted metal that bound those vows?" Wide-eyed, Finn looked at his finger and the gold and silver band wrapped around it. "She could not break our vow. Vanquish you? Yes, but that just sent you right here to me into this lovely little bottle." Dante's voice went cruel. "I can summon you out whenever I need or want you." Finn cringed. "You're mine forever!"

Cowering, Finn asked, "What are you going to do with me now?"

"Whatever I want," Dante answered. "Whatever I want." Dante's eye moved away from the opening.

CHAPTER 33

D IEGO STEPPED OFF THE ELEVATOR into his penthouse apartment to find Juan Carlos waiting for him in the living room. "Thank you for your help tonight." Diego leaned down and kissed Juan Carlos on the cheek. "Where's Alex?"

"He's making sure all the video of tonight is scrubbed." Juan Carlos motioned to the seat across from him. "Please, sit." Diego sat without question. "Aaron got word that someone broke Dr. Wyatt and Jimmy out of the medical jail."

Diego fought the urge to jump from his seat and into action. "What? When? How?"

"He's not sure, but it was in the last twenty-four hours." Juan Carlos shook his head and let out an exasperated sound. "The security cameras and backups were wiped for that time period."

Diego closed his eyes and began rubbing his temples. "They were heavily sedated and under armed guard. It makes no sense."

"Aaron thinks the right people were bribed because the guards assigned to them weren't even working that night." Juan Carlos leaned forward. "There's more."

Diego scoffed. "More? What more can there be?"

"That project I have Alex working on, it's to find a way to neutralize that hypnosis machine Dr. Gingerman invented." Juan Carlos braced himself for the outrage. "It was stolen the same night Dr. Wyatt stole those chemicals from the warehouse."

Diego thought for a moment. "That piece of junk? We removed the hard drive with the programming, and to be on the safe side, I removed the motherboard and sabotaged the power so that it shorts out if anyone tries to activate it."

"Diego Sanz." Juan Carlos fell back in relief. "Do you know how worried I've been about that thing?"

Diego laughed softly. "I can imagine. Look, we defeated the demon twink tonight, freed his minions, and rescued his hostage. I'm going to count that as a win for now. We can worry about Dr.

Wyatt and Timmy in the morning. Right now, I just want to go grab Alex and head to bed."

"Sit," Juan Carlos ordered when Diego went to get up. "He's mad at you. Something about asking him if he'd mind if you brought an asexual dragon into your relationship and then you riding a fairy. I'm assuming we're not talking about a ferryboat."

Exasperated, Diego fell back in his chair. "I was kidding about the asexual dragon." He thought for a second. "It would be cool, though. Can you imagine telling people you're in a throuple and then introducing them to your asexual dragon third?"

"Diego," Juan Carlos warned, then admitted, "it would be really cool."

Diego leaned forward. "Right? But I was only joking. I'm a one-man guy."

"The fairy?" Juan Carlos asked.

Diego shook his head. "He was the hostage. He flew me down the building so we didn't have to fight our way out."

"Makes sense." Juan Carlos thought about it. "You should do something to make him feel special. Maybe take him on a romantic getaway somewhere."

Diego shook his head. "You know how he is about me buying him things."

"This isn't buying him something, but I see your point." Juan Carlos snapped his fingers. "It'll be my treat. My thank you for all the hard work he's done."

Diego went to get up again. "If there isn't anything else..." Diego saw the look on Juan Carlos's face and sat back down. "What now?"

"Aaron decided to run for police chief with Felipe Montoya." Juan Carlos gave him a regretful look. "We have a meeting with them tomorrow morning."

Diego thought about it for a moment. "You said that name sounded familiar. Did you ever figure it out?"

"With everything going on, I completely forgot." Juan Carlos admitted. His phone buzzed with a text message. Reading it, he told Diego, "Clear your schedule for tomorrow night. We're going to In Between to see if the curse is finally broken."

Diego stood up. "Well, if that's everything, I'm going to go find Alex and show him how sexy I find him."

"This is so weird," Dion said. She was sitting at the conference table with Diego on one side and Juan

Carlos on the other. "Are you sure I'm supposed to be here?"

Juan Carlos patted her hand. "You're going to be the COO. You need to get used to these kinds of meetings."

"Do what I do, just nod a lot and do whatever Dion tells you." Diego thought about what he had said. "That's not going to work here, is it?"

Juan Carlos laughed. "No, and it's what I used to do, too."

"Are you two serious?" Dion shook her head.

"Only for the social responsibility stuff," Diego defended. "We normally had you do all the research before the meeting."

"The meetings were just formalities," Juan Carlos added.

Dion shook her head again. "So, the two of you know nothing about Felipe Montoya or his platform?"

Juan Carlos and Diego looked at each other before answering together, "No."

There was a knock on the door, then Aaron appeared in the doorway. "Hey guys, are you ready for us?"

"Come on in." Juan Carlos beamed.

Aaron stepped into the conference room. "Great. Everyone, I'd like you to meet Felipe Montoya."

A young, slender man the same age as Diego stepped in. Juan Carlos studied his baby face. With his curly chestnut hair and kind green eyes, Juan Carlos was certain he knew the man standing nervously before them in an ill-fitting suit. He just couldn't place from where.

"Thank you so much for seeing us." Felipe swallowed hard. "I've really been looking forward to this meeting. No matter how this turns out."

"The pleasure is ours." Juan Carlos stood and stuck out his hand. "You look familiar. Do I know you?"

With a shaky hand, Filipe took the offered hand. "I'm told I look a lot like my father." He nervously looked Juan Carlos in the eyes when he said, "I'm so happy to finally meet you. I believe you know my mother, Lupe Montoya." Juan Carlos's eyes widened. "There's no easy way to say this, so here goes. I'm your son."

The room went silent. Juan Carlos held tightly onto the man's hand.

"Okay, am I the only one who's going to ask it?" Dion asked, breaking the silence. "Fine." She said after looking around at the stunned men "Juan Carlos, how the Hell do you have a son that none of us know about?"

CHAPTER 34

"SO, YOU HAVE A SON," ESMERELDA said, slipping into the booth across from Juan Carlos and Aaron. "Why didn't you ever tell me?"

Juan Carlos knew this talk was coming. He reached under the table to take Aaron's hand. The hurt of the story still hadn't dulled. He doubted it ever would. Aaron gave his hand a reassuring squeeze. He hoped telling this story would get easier the more he told it.

"The abbreviated version is I was eighteen, Lupe was twenty-two, and her student visa was about to expire," Juan Carlos began. "She told me she needed someone to marry her so she could stay in the country."

"Except it wasn't, and she didn't," Aaron added.

"Yes." Juan Carlos closed his eyes to quell his anger. "Her mother was pressuring her to get married. She still wanted to party."

"Marry a young gay man and get both." Esmeralda nodded. "Of course, then her mother pressured her to have children."

"Exactly," Juan Carlos responded.

Esmerelda averted her eyes before asking, "So did you sleep with her?"

"Do you really want to know how the chorizo was made?" Juan Carlos responded bluntly.

Esmeralda nodded. "Good point."

"Anyway. After Filipe was born, Lupe expected us to be this happy little family," Juan Carlos continued. "I was there for my son, but she expected me to be her actual husband. I wouldn't do it. I couldn't. We eventually got divorced, and she made it her mission to ruin my life and prevent me from seeing my son."

Esmerelda raised an eyebrow. "She did understand you are gay? Right?"

"I thought so," Juan Carlos shrugged. "Well, one day, I went to pick up my son and found they had moved out. Her neighbor told me she moved back home." Juan Carlos shook his head in disbelief. "I thought they meant Colombia. She moved back home with her mother. Until today, I never knew she was really a citizen."

Wide-eyed, Esmerelda covered her mouth in shock. "No me diga."

"I searched Colombia for years looking for them when it turns out they were across the city." Juan Carlos snorted. "Of course, I was looking for Felipe Sanz and Lupe Sanz. It never occurred to me that she didn't take my last name, or that she didn't give him mine. I trusted her with all the paperwork. He grew up thinking I was dead, because I was dead to her."

Leaning forward across the table, Esmerelda asked, "How did he find out about you?"

"The first thing his campaign manager did was run a background check on him. That's when he found out the truth." Juan Carlos gave Aaron's hand a squeeze. "He confronted his mother, and she finally came clean last night."

Esmerelda pointed at Aaron and Juan Carlos. "Did he know?"

"Coincidence." Aaron laughed.

Juan Carlos fluttered his hand around as he spoke. "Of course, we're going to do the blood test to make sure, but in my heart, I know it's true."

Esmerelda fell back into the booth. "This is better than a telenovela."

"Speaking of telenovelas," Juan Carlos nodded over to where Diego was talking to Freddy, "how do you think Diego is going to take it?"

Aaron cocked an eyebrow. "Take what?"

"Salvador is an untrained Siren." Esmeralda sighed. "He could hurt someone if he doesn't learn to use his powers. He and Freddy are going to the only place that can train him."

"No! Diego!" Freddy said firmly. "Lobo cannot take his squeaky toys with him!"

Diego stuck his bottom lip out in an exaggerated pout. "But he likes the squeaky toys I got him."

Freddy rolled his eyes. "Lobo says he doesn't like them, but don't get rid of them in case he comes back for a visit."

"See, I told you." Diego smiled triumphantly.

"Seriously, man. Thank you for everything." Freddy put his hand on Diego's shoulder. "You've really been like a brother to me. That's why I wanted to be the one to tell you..."

Diego's look grew serious. "Tell me what?"

"Salvador is an untrained Siren." Freddy looked over at Salvador talking to Alex. "He has to get trained, and the only place he can do that is Atlantis."

Diego's eyes grew wide. "Atlantis is real? Can we go? Are there fish people like in the movies?"

"No, and no." Freddy laughed. "Atlantis exists in a pocket dimension, and when Salvador goes to train, I'm going with him."

Diego's voice cracked when he asked, "How long will you be gone? Will you come back and visit?"

"I don't know, and yes." Freddy looked longingly at Salvador. "I've waited countless lifetimes to be with him. I don't want to spend any more time without him."

"I get it. I just want you to be happy." Diego pulled Freddy into a hug. "I'll make sure to terrorize Esmerelda for you."

Freddy laughed. "Be Careful. She really can give you a tail."

Seeing Salvador by himself, Alex decided to keep him company. "Hi, Salvador. I'm Alex," he said, extending his hand. "How are you doing?"

Taking Alex's hand, he said, "Great, actually." He laughed. "As strange as all this is, you know, being raised by a mystical dead woman, having lived like a dozen lives, dreaming about Freddy, and finding out I'm a Siren, it oddly seems normal."

"That's actually probably the most normal thing that has happened over the past couple of days," Alex joked. "Well, in case no one else has done it yet, let me formally welcome you to the family. I look forward to getting to know you."

Salvador raised an eyebrow. "They didn't tell you?"

"Tell me what?" Alex asked, concerned.

Salvador glanced over at Freddy and Diego, hugging, then back at Alex. "Freddy is coming with me to Atlantis so I can learn how to use my Siren abilities."

"Oh, but you'll be back, right?" Alex glanced over at Diego and Freddy.

"Of course," Salvador answered. "Who wants to live in an ancient mythological paradise city for the rest of their lives?"

"Right?" Alex laughed, then grew serious. "Take care of him, and make sure you come back for a visit as soon as you can."

"I will." Salvador sighed. "We will."

Demona spoke to Gato in hushed tones at the bar. "There's whispers in the community about everything that happened last night."

"Good or bad?" Gato asked.

"Both." Demona looked over her shoulder at Esmerelda. "They are scared of her." She looked over at Diego and Freddy. "The fairy queen is singing their praises."

Gato thought for a moment. "Why is he a queen and not a king?"

"Because fairies like to be different." Demona shrugged. "They're also unsure about you and upset that I let an untrained Siren work at the bar."

Gato nodded. "We need to show them that we're not their enemies. Is that why Ryuu and Herc aren't here?"

"Ryuu had a date with a unicorn, and Herc wanted to visit his family." Demona turned around to look at the occupants of the bar. "Where is that Cotto at?"

Turning around, Gato said, "Ready to get rid of us already?"

"I'll skin you alive if you repeat this." Demona allowed herself a slight smile. "I like you guys. Even the mortals. Especially that Alex guy. He has a very nice aura."

Gato and Demona shielded their eyes when a bright light materialized in the middle of the bar. The light faded to reveal Cotto hovering in the middle of the bar. Lowering his arm, Gato said, "I guess it's time to do this."

Everyone gathered around the hovering orb. Alex put a reassuring hand on Salvador's shoulder. Diego pulled Freddy into a bear hug. Juan Carlos took Esmerelda's left hand while Aaron took her right. Gato and Demona looked at each other and then at Cotto. A pinprick of light formed above Cotto and then grew and solidified into a glowing white stone about half the size of Cotto.

"Salutations." Cotto pulsed. "I apologize for being tardy, but there is a complication that was brought to our attention."

Freddy snarled with a hint of Lobo in his voice, "What complication?"

"Lobo's magic seems to have seeped into Federico's soul," Cotto explained. "He'll still be able to transform without Lobo bonded to his soul."

"They'll be separate, though?" Esmerelda asked, hopefully. "He'll be able to control when and where, right?"

Cotto pulsed twice. "Yes. He will technically be a Lunar Wolf, but also human. Can you live with that?"

"Yes! I'll do anything for my love!" Freddy shouted. He looked over at Salvador. "I'll be anything for him."

Cotto and the created orb swapped places. "Gitana, since you were the one that changed the curse, you must touch the orb first." Letting go of Juan Carlos's and Aaron's hands, she stepped forward and placed her right hand on the orb. Liquid light engulfed her hand.

"Now, Salvador, please." Alex gave him a nod, then Salvador stepped forward and placed his right hand on the orb. His hand was also surrounded by the liquid light. "Now," Cotto pulsed, "Freddy. Whatever you do, do not let go."

Freddy stepped forward and placed his hand on the orb. This time the liquid light did not stop at his hand; it engulfed him. The smaller orb pulsed slowly at first, then started blinking rapidly. The liquid light slowly pulled away from Freddy, then from Esmerelda and Salvador. The light began to swirl in the orb.

The three maintained their connection to the orb despite the blinding, blinking light. Then the smaller orb stopped pulsing and lowered to hover just a foot off the ground. It began expanding, taking the form of a sleek, elegant wolf the size of a pony with silvery blue fur and crystal blue eyes. The three dropped their hands.

"It's nice to have my body to myself," Lobo said, wagging his tail.

Freddy dropped down and hugged the mighty wolf. "Same here."

"You're part of my pack now, you know." Lobo nuzzled Freddy.

Cotto pulsed above them. "I hate to ruin this tender moment, but I must take Lobo back to Lunaray immediately."

"I'll miss you, you big furball." Esmerelda joined in the hug.

"Don't be a stranger," Gato said, putting his arms around the three. "Come visit."

"I will, and you guys come visit me." Lobo sniffled.

"Thank you for not mauling me," Alex teased.

Lobo chuckled. "You're welcome." Lobo turned his head to look at everyone. "Thank you, all of you. You're all a part of my pack now."

Lobo raised his head and howled. Cotto lowered himself to touch Lobo's nose. The two glowed brightly, then exploded in a ball of light, leaving the three kneeling on the floor, hugging each other.

Wiping a tear from his eye, Freddy stood. He looked at Salvador. He took a hesitant step forward. "I waited lifetimes for this."

"Me, too." Salvador stepped toward Freddy.

They stood there, both hesitant to take that next step. Alex groaned. "Kiss already." He pushed Salvador into Freddy's arms.

"I guess we should." Salvador laughed.

Freddy grinned. "Most definitely." Freddy pressed his lips to Salvador's.

CHAPTER 35

"**S**UCK IT IN," DIEGO SAID, PULLING the laces of Juan Carlos's corset.

Through clenched teeth, Juan Carlos snapped, "I am. Pull harder. I'm on in a few minutes."

"A little more." Diego quickly tied the ends of the laces together. "There."

Juan Carlos turned to look at himself in the mirror. "I've changed my mind. I'm not going on."

"The Hell you aren't." Diego panted. "I did not develop those outfits, endure hours of you rehearsing, and just squeeze you into that corset to not have you go on."

Diego picked up a Shadow Guardian suit disc off the makeup table and attached it to Juan Carlos's chest. He double-tapped the center, activating the microbots. The tiny black machines spread across Juan Carlos to create a black ball gown with a blue ribbon of color starting at his left shoulder, then spiraling down to the floor.

"Besides," Diego said proudly, "you're not going on. Dolores Savaje is."

Juan Carlos straightened his shoulders. "That's right. I'm fierce and fabulous."

"And fun in the sack," Aaron said, coming around the corner. He carefully kissed Juan Carlos on the cheek. "I wanted to check on you and let you know I made it."

Juan Carlos adjusted Aaron's tie. "Are you nervous? You're making your big announcement tonight."

"In front of all these people, including the mayor and police chief." Aaron laughed. "Make sure you get a video of their faces."

Diego smiled. "Oh, I will."

"Before I forget," Aaron shook his finger at Diego, "remember that security guard that got kidnapped, Joshua? He's missing. Do you think it's tied to the Dr. Wyatt and Jimmy escape?"

Diego shook his head. "No, he seemed to have a thing for Teddy, err Timmy."

"Enough shop talk," Juan Carlos proclaimed. "Go! Go! Take your seats! I'm about to go on."

"How is he?" Alex asked when Diego sat down.

He leaned over and kissed Alex on the cheek. "Nervous. I wish Freddy were here to see this. He's dedicating the first performance to him."

"I wish I could have met him before he left," Felipe commented. "Where did he go again?"

Diego and Alex shared a look, then Diego answered, "Atlanta. His boyfriend had to go there for training."

"He just met the guy, right?" Felipe asked.

Aaron spoke up, "Sort of."

"It's complicated," Alex added.

Everyone grew quiet and turned their attention to the stage when Esmerelda's voice came over the speakers. "Ladies, gentlemen, gender-fluid, and non-binary people, it is my pleasure to present to you, making her comeback appearance, Dolores Savaje!" Esmerelda stepped off stage and Juan Carlos stepped on stage.

CHAPTER 36

JOSHUA GROANED. HIS HEAD pounded. He felt weak, and his body ached. Everything was blurry when he opened his eyes. "Here, drink this." He heard a deep voice say. His head was lifted up. Something was pressed to his lips, and cool sweet water splashed into his dry, cotton mouth.

Joshua tried to blink the blurry away. He could make out the dark outline of a stocky man with a beard leaning over him. "Teddy?" Joshua choked out.

Joshua felt a wet towel brush against his forehead. "No," the deep voice said. "I was looking for him when I came across you."

Joshua's vision began to clear. He saw a shirtless, rugged lumberjack of a man with a full jet-black beard. "What happened to Teddy?" Joshua's voice cracked when he spoke.

"I don't know. I went to his cave to bring him his medicine and check on him. When I got there, he was gone," the man said, continuing to wipe the wet towel over Joshua's face. "It looked like there was some sort of fight."

"I need to go find him." Joshua made to get up, but a rough, calloused hand pressed him back down.

"Hold on. You're in no shape to go anywhere anytime soon. You've been passed out in my cabin for the last three days." The man began running the cold towel over Joshua's neck and chest. "It looks like you took a bad spill and hit your head."

Joshua tried to remember. Flashes came to him, getting lost in the woods, shivering on the forest floor at night, running out of food and water, then stumbling and rolling down that hill. "I'm okay." Joshua tried to get up, but the hand pressed him back down. "Who are you?"

"I'm Jack," the man answered. "Teddy's boyfriend."

RECIPE

A LRIGHT, EVERYONE, IT'S RECIPE time. In the beginning of Shadow Guardian and the Big Bad Wolf, Esmerelda makes everyone tortilla Espanola. Now, this is something of a staple in Spanish cooking. It's cheap to make, feeds a lot of people and can be eaten for days after.

My mother used to make them at least once a week for the family. I still use the same old lid to flip the tortilla. Now, in the story, Alex is confused when he sees the tortilla Espanola because it's not what you think of when you think of tortilla. Tortilla Espanola is a mix of egg and potatoes and is sort of like a frittata.

Tortilla Espanola

What you need:
  Four to five potatoes, peeled and diced.
  Four large eggs
  Two to three cups of oil of your choice
  Salt and pepper to taste.
  Two frying pans.
  Two plates
  Two mixing bowls.
  A spatula
  A slotted spatula

Optional:
  Onion.

This is going to be a recipe for one tortilla Espanola. You're going to need about four to five good size potatoes. You're going to peel them; then you're going to dice them up into small pieces and in various shapes. You do want them to be thicker than your pinky. It's okay if they are thin, but if they are thicker, you'll have to fry them longer.

Next, you're going to put your diced potatoes in a saltwater bath while you heat up your oil to between 350 and 400 degrees. If you're having anything else, like bacon or sausage with the tortilla Espanola, this is an excellent time to start those. When the oil is hot enough, strain out just enough potatoes and add them to the oil.

BE CAREFUL! Do not just put the potatoes from the saltwater bath into the oil. You will get burned by splattering oil. Do not overcrowd the pan or deep fryer you're using. Take your time. These will have to cool, so it's better to take your time than get burned.

When the potatoes are slightly golden brown, go ahead and remove them from the oil. I put them on a paper towel bed to soak up any extra oil and cool. When they are cool, transfer them into a big mixing bowl and wait for the rest of the potatoes. This is when you can add extra stuff. Try to stick with dry things. I add diced onion to mine.

Now you're going to add three dashes of salt and three dashes of pepper. Put your tortilla pan on the stove on medium-high heat. I'll explain the tortilla pan in a bit. Add four large eggs to the potatoes and then begin mixing. This is why you have to let the potatoes cool first; you don't want them cooking the eggs.

A tortilla pan is a real thing, but I don't use one. Some places actually sell this contraption. You don't need that. What you need is a medium size frying pan that you can fit a plate over. Preferably the one you're going to serve it from.

Why? Because we're going to test your hand-eye coordination

Okay, your pan is hot. Your eggs and potatoes are mixed. Time for them to meet. Pour your tortilla mix into the pan. Use a spatula to scrape the bowl and even out the tortilla. Run the spatula around the rim of the tortilla to keep it from sticking, and be patient.

Depending on the thickness of your tortilla, you're going to let it cook for ten to fifteen minutes. You're going to be tempted to turn up the heat. DON'T. All you'll do is burn the outside and leave the inside raw. Just be patient and watch it as it cooks along the sides.

Now the bottom is cooked. Take a plate, or old pot lid like I do, and put it on top of the pan, covering the entire thing. You've seen people do this with cakes, sort of. Flip the tortilla onto the plate. Then you're going to carefully slide the now uncooked bottom back into the pan to cook the rest.

Use your spatula to carefully tuck down the sides while the top cooks. This can be anywhere from five to ten minutes, depending on how runny you like it. Fifteen minutes if you want the eggs cooked all the way through. You can test it by feeling in the center of the tortilla. The firmer the feel, the more it is cooked.

Now one last flip onto the plate, and you are done! Cut and yell for everyone to come and get it. I usually serve this with bacon and sausage. Any leftover tortilla can be refrigerated and served for up to two days. You can eat it hot or cold. I prefer my leftover tortilla (if there is any) hot with ketchup.

My mother made the best tortilla Espanolas. The lid I use to flip my tortillas is the same one she used. In fact, it used to be the lid of the pot she made puchero in. The lid is actually older than I am. Using that lid is a connection with my mother. I can feel her guiding me through each of the steps. So do my mother proud when you make a tortilla Espanola.

It does take time and practice to get it right with the flip, but it doesn't matter what it looks like. It all tastes the same. One of the proudest moments of my life was when I made my first tortilla Espanola. I actually made it for my mother, and it came out almost perfectly. It just needed more salt.

BOOK CLUB QUESTIONS

1. Freddy and Salvador would be what you consider soulmates. Do you believe that you are destined to be with a particular person? Why?

2. Diego says he wasn't planning on telling Alex that he's Shadow Guardian. Do you agree with this decision?

3. Elias speaks their truth in the story, and they feel a surge of power. Do you think speaking their truth helped empower them?

4. When Salvador goes to leave the audition at In Between, he tells Demona all the reasons he didn't get the job. Do you think we automatically assume the worst when the person doesn't react the way we expect?

5. After everything Dante and Finn have been through, do you think he's still manipulating Finn, or do you think he truly loves him?

6. Juan Carlos decides to leave DJC so he can pursue his own passions and life. If you could, what passion would you follow?

7. Alex gets mad at Diego when he buys him expensive clothes without telling him. Do you think Alex has a right to be mad that Diego did this, regardless of Diego's intentions?

8. Is Finn a villain, or is he a victim that thinks he's a villain?

9. Diego says he was only joking about a throuple with Ryuu, but it seems to bother Alex. If your partner asked you about being in a throuple, how would you react?

10. Esmerelda and Gato have a complicated history. If you were Gato, could you forgive Esmerelda for just writing and not visiting, even though Gato says he didn't want her to see him in prison?

Author Bio

Robby Lewis is a writer based out of Charleston, South Carolina. When he's not busy with his plants, being a doggy-daddy, or watching the latest Sci-Fi, he can be found coming up with new stories for his readers. He's influenced by such writers as T.J. Klune, Rhys Ford, Jordan Castillo Price, and L.A. Witt. You can keep up with Robby Lewis's latest releases and antics on his social media at https://robert-j-lewis.com/

MORE BOOKS FROM 4 HORSEMEN PUBLICATIONS

LGBT ROMANCE

AJ BUCHANNAN
Orchestrated Love

ESKAY KABBA
Hidden Love
Not So Hidden
Signs of Affection
Deeply Devoted to Him
Honest Love
A Plane and Simple Connection

LUCAS LAMONT
Roman's Reckoning: Type 6
Mikaél's Moment: Type 6
Stephan's Resurgence: Type 5
Anastasia's Arrival: Type 6

STORMIE SKYES
Check Yes, No, or Maybe

V.C. WILLIS
The Prince's Priest
The Priest's Assassin
The Assassin's Saint
The Champion's Lord

FANTASY, SCIFI, & PARANORMAL ROMANCE

AMANDA FASCIANO
Waking Up Dead
Dead Vessel
The Dead Show
Dead Revelations

BEAU LAKE
The Beast Beside Me
The Beast Within Me
Taming the Beast: Novella
The Beast After Me
Charming the Beast: Novella

The Beast Like Me
An Eye for Emeralds
Swimming in Sapphires
Pining for Pearls

CHELSEA BURTON DUNN
By Moonlight
Moonbound
Bloodthirsty